City of Orphans

CITY OF ORPHANS

PATRICIA ROBERTSON

The Porcupine's Quill, Inc.

CANADIAN CATALOGUING IN PUBLICATION DATA

Robertson, Patricia.
  City of orphans

ISBN 0-88984-176-4

I. Title

PS8585.024C5 1994   C813'.54   C94-930804-8
PR9199.3.R62C5 1994

Published by The Porcupine's Quill, Inc., 68 Main Street, Erin, Ontario NOB 1TO with financial assistance from The Canada Council and the Ontario Arts Council. The support of the Government of Ontario through the Ministry of Culture, Tourism and Recreation is also gratefully acknowledged.

Represented in Canada by the Literary Press Group. Trade orders available from General Distribution Services in Canada (Toronto) and the United States (Niagara Falls). Selected titles also available from Inland Book Company.

Some of these stories, in slightly different versions, have previously appeared or will appear in *The Second Macmillan Anthology, Quarry, Canadian Fiction Magazine, The Northern Review, New: West Coast Fiction,* and *Writing North: An Anthology of Contemporary Yukon Writers.*

Readied for the press by John Metcalf.
Copy edited by Doris Cowan.

Cover is after the painting 'Night Windows', Edward Hopper, 1928, oil on canvas (73.7 x 86.4 cm). The Museum of Modern Art. Gift of John Hay Whitney. Photograph © 1993, The Museum of Modern Art, New York.

CONTENTS

For my mother,
and in memory of my father

and for all my teachers

RIDING TO THE CORRIDA

SATURDAYS DARLA AND MICAELA hitched downtown and stood in the video arcades, not playing but watching the slim-hipped boys bent over the machines. It was Darla's idea to watch, Darla who ran red lipstick over her mouth and stood with a hip thrust out in the gloom where the machines hummed. Micaela hung back, shook her bangs in her eyes and stuffed her hands in the sleeves of her jean jacket. Later they wandered through the department stores, leaning into mirrors to hold earrings at their ears, turning their heads this way and that. Sometimes Darla slipped into a change-room with a pair of lacy French-cut panties and came back with her own cast-off pair on the hanger. Micaela pretended to be looking at nightgowns.

At fifteen Darla's plump arms already left an afterglow when they moved through the air. Beside her Micaela was a dark elf. When they sat on concrete planters on the street mall Micaela hugged her knees to her chest and let Darla deflect the force of the men's stares with the bounce of her ponytail. Darla did not seem to notice; she applied blue eyeliner, freshly stolen. In between strokes she talked about the stepfather with his leather belt, the four younger sisters, the mother who sagged in the background, the boy she had slept with at twelve. Micaela listened. There were no echoes in her own house where her mother's mouth had swallowed her father's name. Her ears swelled with Darla's secrets. In gratitude Darla eased from the department stores the earrings and bracelets their limited money would not buy.

They stood on a downtown street, thumbs out. Darla counted makes of cars, the top lines: fifteen Cadillacs, five Porsches, three Jaguars, a Daimler. Micaela kept track of colours: maroon, taupe, metallic grey. This one will stop, I know it, Darla said, or: See that dark blue Rolls with the silver trim? That one for sure. As the cars glided past, sometimes carrying a man's smiling face or pink-tongued mouth, Darla wriggled her fingers after them. May your wheels fall off at the next stoplight, she said. May your radiator uncurl. May your engine block melt.

When the cream Chevrolet stopped and the back door swung open, Darla jumped, Micaela crept in. The driver laid a pearl-cuffed arm on the back of his seat. Black hair, white teeth, about as old as a father. I am lost, he said. You can help? I look for *el parque*.

Sure, said Darla. You Spanish? My friend speaks Spanish.

Micaela pressed herself against the seat. Her palms were moist. Only a year of high school Spanish, she said.

My name is Juan Carlos, he said, nosing out into traffic. *Como el rey*.

Something about the king, whispered Micaela. Maybe he's related.

At the entrance to the park the fountains played, cherry blossoms scattered across the hood of the car. Beautiful, very beautiful, said Juan Carlos. He parked the car near the zoo. They walked in the sunshine from the seals to the orangutans. Juan Carlos bought a bag of popcorn and took a photograph of Darla kneeling on the ground feeding a squirrel out of her hand. *Ahora te toca a ti*, he said, motioning to Micaela. She squinted into the sun, shading her eyes. Maybe later, by the totem pole, she said. Darla jumped up, giggling, and threw her arm round Micaela's shoulders, her bare knees pocked with gravel. Ah, that is nice, said Juan Carlos, and bent down to take the picture.

They stood on the outdoor chess board where the wooden figures were almost as large as Micaela. Darla was the white queen and Micaela was the black. Juan Carlos moved the pieces. *Los peones*, he said, have nothing. Like in life. *El caballero* stamps them in the dust. He replaced Micaela's pawn with Darla's knight. And *el obispo*, he is a man of God yet he too eats them up. Another pawn fell. But *la reina*, she is the most powerful, she can do anything she wants. He pushed Micaela forward by the shoulders and rolled a white pawn from her path. She would have thrown coins and cakes from her castle balcony. In that sunlight gold coins spun and glittered towards the cobblestones below.

On the way back to the car he gave them each his card. Micaela traced the raised letters with her fingers. Juan Carlos Ramírez Solano, Comerciante y Representante. Calle Tomás Socorro, 17, Barcelona. I am a businessman, he said. Import-export. Clothes, shoes, textiles. And oranges? said Micaela. Her mother had spoken of hitch-hiking years ago along dusty roads past dark trees with golden fruit. Juan Carlos laughed. It is true, he said. Seville oranges, for *mermelada*. But no, I do not have.

Are you married? said Darla. Yes, he said, four children, the oldest is fourteen. María del Carmen. *Te parece a ti*, he said, touching Micaela on the arm. The hair is different, but the eyes are the same. He's a smoothie, said Darla in an undertone.

You have been most kind, he said. Can I invite you to take coffee with me? He still looked crisp and fresh in his grey suit with the small lace triangle over his heart. He held out his arms for them to take. Micaela's fingers touched the smooth grey cloth. Was this what a father did, walked arm in arm with his daughters to have coffee in a fancy restaurant? Her name was María del Carmen, and she looked up smiling at her father's handsome face.

He watched them in the rear-view as they drove out of the park, the blonde one, *la rubia*, bouncing up and down in her seat and the little dark one, *la morenita*, sitting back quietly against the red plush. *La rubia* might be sixteen or seventeen, it was hard to tell with her red mouth and blue-fringed eyes. The other one was probably the age of Mari-Carmen, looking lost and fragile in her oversize jean jacket. Where were the parents that they allowed their daughters to wander the streets and catch rides with strangers? He could take them to the distant mountains, or far south into Mexico, and who would ever find them? The world was vast and a child small and easily mislaid. And then no longer a child. He guided the car carefully into the main flow of traffic.

Tell me about yourselves, he said over the silver tea service on the marble-topped table. They sat under glass beside windows that almost spilled them into the harbour. A waiter in white gloves brought the pastry tray. Darla chose something that oozed chocolate and custard, but Micaela hesitated among the pastels of the petit fours. Juan Carlos took a slice of lemon with the little silver tongs.

Darla talked, licking her fingers at the end of sentences. Micaela listened. The man opposite her flew over blue oceans and wore pearl cufflinks and lifted silver tongs under a roof whose colour changed with the weather. How could she tell him about the cramped house on the east side, her mother in her red-and-white checkout girl uniform, the father who was only a faded smile from a summer fifteen years ago? This man had beautiful daughters who wore crisp navy uniforms and white knee-socks like the girls who went to the Catholic high school. On Saturdays, he said, he took his family out for *la merienda*, coffee and pastries in one of the cafés on the Ramblas. While she and Darla stole.

I fly back tomorrow, he was saying to Darla. Just in time for the spring *feria* in Seville. Do you know it? It is very famous, people come from all over the world.

Darla wriggled forward, Micaela leaned her chin in her hands. Juan Carlos pulled up a razor-creased pant leg as he crossed one knee over the other. At the height of the sun, he said, the *caballeros* rode through the streets to the fairground in their short jackets and wide-brimmed hats, their ladies mounted behind them side-saddle in flounced dresses and lace mantillas. From striped tents waiters rushed forward with glasses of pale gold *manzanilla* for the thirsty riders. Under the paper lanterns plump grandmothers and tiny girls danced *la sevillana*, their dresses frothing. The match and water sellers cried Fire! Water! while the guitarists threw back their corded necks and sang. And punctually at five, every afternoon, the bullfight, *la corrida*, began.

Darla wrinkled her nose. Ugh, she said, I wouldn't go. Juan Carlos shrugged. There is a great respect for the bull, he said. It is difficult to explain. It is like a dance, a dance with no mercy where every step must be exact. Where the *torero* wraps the bull around him like a dress.

But it's not fair, said Darla. My brother, said Juan Carlos, was training to be a *torero*. A bull caught him right here – he pressed his fingers to his groin – during a *farol*, a pass of the cape. They could not stop the bleeding. He was twenty.

In the silence the waiter appeared with fresh hot water. As the steam rose into the air the bull's flanks heaved, its neck with the gay *banderillas* glossy with blood. It pawed the ground in the turning sun. The *torero* drew his sword and sighted along it. The lady in the president's box stilled her fan. The *torero* ran forward, thrust the sword deep into the bull's hump, and leapt clear of the horns. The bull stood motionless, feet splayed, staggered and fell. Hats, scarves, flowers sailed into the air. The *torero* stood cap in hand with his cape over his arm and saluted the lady in the president's box.

If you were a lady riding horseback to the bullfight, Juan Carlos said, looking at Micaela, the men would say *piropos* as you passed by. Compliments like *guapa, linda, hermosa*. I might say to you – and he swept an imaginary hat from his head to his heart – *qué ojos más lindos!*

What? said Darla.

I am inviting you and the señorita with the pretty eyes to dinner, he said.

I better phone my mom, said Darla. Tell her I'm okay.

In the cream Chevrolet they rode down a street where glass store-fronts sparkled, people sipped coffee at white tables, men in flowing coats strode past women in high heels. Down to where the street almost dipped into the sea, then rounded the curve of the bay. People walked, biked, jogged with children, dogs, baby strollers. Juan Carlos and the girls walked under the chestnut trees. A red-and-yellow kite sailed over their heads. A man in a suit played a clarinet, the breeze ruffling the pages on his music stand.

We never rode in a cream Chevy before, said Darla. Black, the last one, and before that blue, and before that – do you remember, Micaela?

Micaela shook her head. You do so! said Darla. Micaela has this fantastic memory. That's why she gets good grades.

And you do not, señorita *caballito*? Juan Carlos tugged her ponytail gently. Darla squealed. I smack boys' hands when they do that, she said. Juan Carlos held his own out, palms up. Go ahead, he said. When Darla brought her hand down he caught and held it, laughing. Darla tugged and squealed. Micaela looked at the blue dissolving mountains.

You're mean, said Darla, standing up and brushing the seat of her skirt. She wandered down to a knot of girls and boys sitting on the seawall. Juan Carlos lay back on the grass and shut his eyes. Micaela sat cross-legged and severed a grass-blade. A ladybug crawled along the upside-down blade and onto her thumb. Fire, whispered Micaela, water. The ladybug remained still. Juan Carlos sat up and pressed his fingers against his eyes. Four days of business, business, business, and I am tired. He laid a hand gently on her shoulder. Are you happy, *morenita*? Micaela coaxed the ladybug back onto the grass-blade and laid it in the grass. I don't know, she said. Juan Carlos stood up and cupped his hands to his mouth. *Oye, niña!* he called. Down at the seawall Darla's blonde head turned as she shaded her eyes and looked up.

A swan of ice sailed down the buffet table, carrying slices of rose and pale green fruit between its wings. Juan Carlos cut meat with his knife and fork and carried the fork to his mouth with his left hand. From time to time he dabbed at his lips with his napkin. Micaela watched his left wrist flex as he raised food to his mouth, then lifted her own. Darla stabbed potato with her right hand.

Half a glass of wine for each of you, said Juan Carlos, pouring. That is what my children have. The wine, a pale honey, tasted like acid on Micaela's tongue. She swallowed, ate some bread, took another sip. In Spain the children drank this wine, sitting solemnly at dinner with their parents. Juan Carlos lifted his glass. *Un brindis*, he said. To friendship. To our countries. To your queen and my king.

Micaela laid down her knife. Have you met him, your king?

she said. At a reception once at a trade fair, said Juan Carlos. He shook my hand. I have a photograph at home.

Was he wearing a crown? asked Darla.

Oh no. He is a very modern king. He even has a pilot's licence.

Micaela looked at her plate. *The King of Spain's daughter, Came to visit me, And all because* ... How did it go? Juan Carlos was talking. *I had a little nut tree, Nothing would it bear, But a silver nutmeg and a golden pear.* Yes, Juan Carlos was saying, the king often travels to other countries. *The King of Spain's daughter, Came to visit me, And all for the sake of my little nut tree.* But without silver nutmegs and golden pears, what hope was there? Still, the hand that had shaken the king's had rested on her own shoulder.

There was a little wine left in the bottle. Juan Carlos held it out. Darla placed her hand over her glass and the wine splashed onto her fingers. She flicked the drops at Juan Carlos, giggling. *Hui, qué cara tienes!* cried Juan Carlos, and snapped his napkin like a *torero*. Micaela tried to remember the Spanish textbook. *Cara* – was that like *cariño*, darling? Darla's ponytail was bouncing, bouncing. Micaela closed her eyes and swallowed her wine.

Juan Carlos was ordering something from the waiter, coffee and a glass of brandy. He drew a cigar out of his inside jacket pocket and tapped one end on the table. The waiter set dishes piled with cream in front of her and Darla. After this most charming evening, said Juan Carlos, I will drive you home.

Oh no, said Darla. We want to see your hotel first. Don't we, Micaela?

After a bottle of wine and two brandies he could not be drunk, but the lights in his room were too bright, the pattern on the carpet blurred. Overtiredness, no doubt. *La rubia* sat on the stool at the dressing table and spun round and round, making him dizzy. And *la morenita*? Ah yes, behind the drapes somewhere, staring out at the city lights. He could not remember why he had brought them here. *La morenita* was so small there was no bulge in the drapes to reveal where she stood. There was a knock at the door. *La rubia* answered it and came back with a bellboy who carried a tray of something. He managed to pull out some coins for a tip. Look what we ordered, said *la rubia*, and showed him a plate of something disgusting, some sort of sauce poured over chips. She held it out to him; he shook his head. Want some, Micaela? she called, chewing. The drapes parted and *la morenita* came into the room.

La rubia held his business card in her greasy fingers. We'll come and visit you, one day, she said. She hitched up her skirt on the side away from him and tucked the card in the top of her panties. In the dressing table mirror he saw the line of round bare thigh scalloped with white lace. He beckoned *la morenita* over, took her wrist. *Dile a tu amiga*, he said, *que es bella*. She looked at him uncertainly. *Bella*, your friend, he said. *Guapa. Hermosa*. His tongue, thick with longing, would not form the English words. *Bella*, he repeated stupidly, which was not what he meant. Butter-soft flesh, melting between his fingers, but he could not explain that to *la morenita*. He traced her baby palm with his finger and kissed it, protectively. *La morenita* pulled away her wrist. Stood up and walked to the other side of the room and disappeared behind the drapes.

From the seventeenth floor all the lights of the city lay before her. Nets and arcs and columns of lights, red, gold, silver. All the lights in the world must be here, far from her own street where the streetlamps were always out. Would the King of Spain's daughter be impressed when she came to visit? She would take her by the hand and show her the cherry trees, the wooden queen as big as herself, the roof that changed colours.

Behind her she heard Darla's voice, hushed, urgent. *Micaela!* She opened the drapes a crack, blinking in the bright light. Juan Carlos lay asleep on the bed, his tie crumpled, one shoe on the floor. Darla's hands dripped with lace, necklaces, cufflinks. There's more in that suitcase, she said, filling Micaela's pockets. You got room down your front too, she said. Hurry up, she said. In the doorway Micaela looked back at the man on the bed, his arm thrown sideways, mouth open.

CITY OF ORPHANS

THERE IS A PLACE near my house where I go in the summer to lie like a lizard and sun myself on the gravestones. I open my shirt and expose my pale chest to the sun. The young boys with the hair in their eyes, they pause in their sauntering and stand near me, rubbing a hip against a mossy headstone. I ignore them, I am there for the sun. Wherever I go I see them, on the beach, in the cafés, at the markets. The smell of warm flesh, or warm metal, attracts them. Preferably both together, and when I had both I spent without mercy, I was pale for lack of daylight, the boys clung to me with mouths open. One of them I loved, delicate bones and lashes like curtains. Peter. Beautiful Peter of the pouting lips. But love like this must be watered by coins, and when the rainy season ended Peter went away, an old story. Now I ignore them. I am here for the sun.

In summer it is crowded. People spread towels on the gravestones and lie down, a layer of living bodies upon the dead. Each of us has our favourite spot. Mine is the grave of Lucy Eliza Severns, who died of diphtheria aged three. I bring flowers on her birthday, a cupcake with a candle. They are always gone the next day. At night this is a city of broken bottles and curses. No one shares with the dead.

To while away the long afternoons I tell Lucy stories. She listens calmly as the wolf gobbles up the grandmother. Her mother and sister, in the next grave, have already died. The wolf is real; the shadows lengthen; Lucy's face pales and vanishes. I shiver and look round. The afternoon sun has gone and everyone has left.

I fasten my pants over my trunks, comb my thinning hair. I walk slowly past the stone angels, the wreathed urns. I linger at the gate and watch as shadows swallow the pillars and the angels take flight. It is only a short distance to my room. I sit in the dark, I drink wine. Is this where I have ended up at fifty, behind doors in an alien city where I talk only to shopkeepers and a dead child?

I keep no photographs in this building whose spine snapped long ago, I thought all was preserved in the amber of sunlight. Peter laughing as he turned to face me, the hair falling in his eyes, or a group of us – Peter, myself, Klaus, the Moroccans – gathered round a café table somewhere, a beach and whitecaps in the distance. We were runaways, we knew better than to try shackling each other's wrists. The world was an orphanage, but we had built our own campfire outside the walls.

I had brought only my small inheritance, my father's books, and a photograph of myself aged seven, my cheeks still damp from a spanking that morning for taking extra marmalade. I sat in cafés with a newspaper on my lap, I strolled on the promenade among tourists with bony knees and large shoulder-bags. I had come there to live, but where was life? I spoke only to beggars and bartenders. The tourists looked at everything through their camera lenses and then flew home. I felt stranded, waiting for a flight that never came.

I took a room in the old quarter with a tiny wrought-iron balcony above the street. In the afternoons I lay there on damp sheets listening to raised voices, fragments of song, the ring of a telephone. I spoke now, haltingly, to the couple who ran the pension, the fruit sellers in the market. I began teaching English at a school where the staff had all shed old selves and were hostile in their nakedness – except for Klaus, who in a former life had thrown all his cameras in the Rhine and left to seek he knew not what. There's a café in the port area, he said to me one day, quite disreputable. Would you like to go?

Perhaps that was where life was, sealed up like a genie among the crumbling houses and the smell of fish. No whites, he said, meaning no tourists, and after classes ended I followed him without looking back.

There is no winter here, only a cloudy season. I visit Lucy to keep her company. Today when I walk past the gatehouse I notice that someone has spread cardboard on the floor. Also a rolled-up blanket, a plastic dog dish, some empty wine bottles. Even with the cardboard the stone floor must be cold and damp. The occupant must have been moved on from somewhere else, one of the beaches perhaps. He is safe here, no one patrols this abandoned place. But I want to seize his belongings and toss them over the railings. Lucy and I are used to our privacy in winter; we do not want to be disturbed.

Look at these cheekbones, said Klaus, who had kept a camera after all to take pictures of beautiful boys. We looked at the photographs he'd taken of one who smiled and pouted and stuck out his tongue. Of course I'll sell them, he said when I asked. Peter would be flattered.

A face full of evil, said one of the Moroccans. They say he started that brawl with the paratroopers. Took off just as the military police arrived.

He says one of the soldiers insulted his mother. Klaus filled up our wine glasses.

When one lives in the gutter, said the Moroccan, one should expect to be pelted with garbage.

Then you're lucky I extricated you from the orange peels, Klaus said, and there would have been another fight if I hadn't intervened. Cheekbones! said the Moroccan. They cast interesting shadows on a pillow – and he spat into the street.

That night I lay in the airless heat of my room listening to the cries of the old quarter, comforting and abrasive as a cat's tongue. What would entice that sulky boy to stand behind shutters at my balcony window while I ran my fingers down his spine? I wanted to see that pink mouth open, the neck arch, hear him cry out as I bit into downy skin. I pressed my face into the pillow but still he stood there, smiling at me from beneath those long lashes. My little life of carefully counted coins, chalky fingers, bottles of wine – the same life I had, in mid-life, left behind me – lay about me like a husk. Peter stood at a doorway visible only in outline, poised to enter, his face turned away from me.

I got up, dressed, and went out. In the first club they'd never heard of him. In the second they were suspicious, in the third they pretended not to understand. I stayed to drink and dance with the prostitutes, and staggered home in an apricot dawn past shopkeepers unrolling their metal store-fronts.

Lucy's saint's day. Even a Protestant child is entitled to a saint's day, surely, in this country, though her father would not approve. The Reverend Thomas Elijah Severns, tall and thin-lipped, I think, in his dog collar and black cassock. What did he have to offer these foreigners in place of bleeding crucifixes and weeping statues? But he lost his wife and two daughters in the diphtheria epidemic of 1893 and died himself ten years later. Only forty-two. Perhaps his faith helped mend the cracks in his heart.

It is raining. I have brought Lucy a card, thick with gilt and glitter. Lucy's namesake was a second-century Christian martyr, walled up alive by the pagan Turks. I place the card on the grave beneath the stone cherub with the missing arm. Already the paper is turning limp, the colours blurring. As I leave, the old dog in the gatehouse lifts its whitened muzzle and looks at me with rheumy eyes. The huddled pile in the corner doesn't stir.

The sulky boy behind shutters laughed at me, the net of sound thickened my tongue. I wandered for hours through narrow streets where the walls fluttered with laundry and pigeons, where women spoke in cracked voices and threw slops at my feet. Food turned to paste in my mouth, even the bougainvillea spilling down walls lost its colour. I saw that couples in the street held hands to mock me.

Peter was leaning against the wall smoking a cigarette when I came out of school one evening. He looked at me, smiling, and the street tilted. When he slipped round the corner I ran after him, but he had vanished. He reappeared at the end of an alleyway, disappeared into darkness, emerged out of a doorway on an intersecting street. Several times I thought I'd lost him in those narrow passages where the sun barely entered. When I came out, blinking, into a sunny square full of palm trees, Peter was sitting beside the statue of a poet and opposite was the street leading to my pension. How had he known? He led me up to my room and waited while I unlocked the door, not looking at me. Inside he fingered everything on my dresser, took the bills I held out, stood looking down into the street while he unbuttoned his shirt. This is what you wanted, isn't it? he said. My mouth was watering, I couldn't speak. Was I dreaming this naked boy behind shutters, or had I called a dream into flesh? No, just stay there, I said as he moved towards the bed. I struggled to remember the word for *stand*. Be still, I said. Be still.

I have taken to walking past the gatehouse every morning on my way back from the market, bringing a soup bone or some meat scraps for the dog. It always comes out to greet me, moving slowly on arthritic legs. Once I tried bringing food for the man, but he pushed it away, muttering. I do not know his name, he will not talk. Perhaps he thinks I will report him to the authorities. When he sees me coming he crouches in the corner and pulls his jacket over his face.

There is a pile of wine bottles now, a shopping cart filled with bags, a rank smell. What does he do all day, this man who has chosen to lie down among the dead? But the dead are always among us, and sometimes they change places with the living and no one notices. Is my own case any different? Will the olive seller in the market miss me when I no longer come to buy his olives?

Peter sprawled nude in a thousand English and Scandinavian photo albums. Medium height, slender, skin the colour of the inside of a walnut shell, teeth sharp as a cat's. Three gold molars in his lower jaw to replace the ones he'd lost in a fight. Said he was eighteen, fifteen, twenty-five, depending on the hearer, the occasion, the weather. His English name, too, was assumed. I had no name before I came here, he said when I asked. At home they called me the scarred one. This because of a knife wound embroidering his left ribs. And before the knife wound? I was born with it, he said. The midwife crossed herself and called my mother a witch. In another version he'd been knifed while defending his sister from rapists. Now his sister was a prostitute and his mother in jail, and his father had drunk lye from the shame of it all. One of the Moroccans, who claimed friends in the secret police, said Peter's wealthy shipping family had thrown him out for selling drugs to the sailors.

All I know is that the skin on the insides of his elbows tasted like ocean, and his smile would have aroused an archbishop.

A colder winter than usual, everyone is saying, an unlikely frost has blighted the tomatoes. In the gatehouse a thin puff of vapour rises in the corner. The old dog follows me at a distance. I am tired of wolves and witches and breadcrumbs; I pull my jacket tighter and try to remember the stories my mother told me. There were princes and swans, swords and dragons, but all the pieces are mixed up. I do not want to disappoint Lucy. I begin a story about a mountain with a jewelled palace on the top and a journey involving a little girl and – what? A dog, of course, as the old dog reaches me, panting, and lies down at my feet. The little girl wraps up bread and cheese and olives in her kerchief and sets out on the journey with her faithful dog. Come back, come back! calls her mother, but the little girl is determined, because they are very poor and if she can find the jewelled palace that everyone talks about they will always have enough to eat and drink. The mother's voice fades in the distance. I bury my hands in my pockets and watch Lucy and the dog trudge up the dusty road and out of sight.

I never knew when Peter would turn up. Sometimes he came at dawn and pulled me out of bed for coffee and fried dough at one of the cafés. Or he arrived in the middle of the night after I hadn't seen him for days and emptied bracelets, earrings, coins from his pockets. Of course they're gifts, he said when I asked, widening his eyes and pouting. I don't need to steal. He laid a thick gold chain across my chest. This one's for you, he said, silencing my protests with a finger. I have nothing else to give you – and he wound a necklace that might have been diamonds round his throat.

I want nothing, I said, but you. I have an appointment, he said, wriggling out of my embrace and gathering up his pirate treasure. Once he left his jacket behind; I drew out handfuls of kroner, yen and American dollars, a pair of lace panties, and the business card of a Mr. Chuck Drayton of Huntsville, Texas.

Once I followed him, panting behind him at a distance as he ran lightly through the dark streets. He vaulted over traffic barriers, leaped up to touch balcony railings. In the club zone I lost him; an eddy of boys drifted in and out of doorways, arguing, flirting, watching. I sat at a bar and drank while a group of sailors bickered in a corner. The boys corralled each foreign woman who entered, tossing their heads and showing their teeth. If she rebuffed them they withdrew, pretended indifference, until a few minutes later one of them circled back, said something, sat down at her table. The trap closed, the lamb smiled at her captor, and a quiver like a sigh ran through the knot of boys as they turned back to the doorway.

How well you speak the language, said the bartender as he refilled my glass. How different you are from the other tourists, said the boys, overhearing us. You have lived here a long time, no?

A few months, I said modestly, and ordered a round. I was swollen with my new knowledge of language and gesture, blind to the knotted undergrowth of folk memory, street smells, cries hurtling down the centuries. They were just boys, children really, friendly and curious as puppies. I bought another round. Where did I come from? Ah, but it was cold there! Was I rich? How well I spoke the language! But I've seen you somewhere, said one of them. I know I've seen you. He snapped his fingers. The café, he said, in the port area, and the laughter stopped as though sliced by a knife.

You prefer the company, said one, of Moroccans and queers?

Aren't you man enough for a woman? said another. They edged forward and crowded me against the bar. Leave him alone, said the bartender, but one of them had seized my arm and others had appeared suddenly from the street. I was pushed forward roughly towards the door. Behind me I heard chairs overturning, shouts, a woman's scream. Out of the corner of my eye I saw a knife flash. We spilled out into the street.

Someone punched me in the ribs and I doubled over and fell. A boot caught me in the small of my back and a bolt of pain raced up my spine. As I staggered to my feet I heard Peter's voice: Get out of here! Get lost! I ran in a half-crouch, blindly, a thick liquid dripping in my eyes – blood, I realized, from a gash on my forehead. At the corner I turned and looked back. Half the street seemed to be in uproar. I staggered on a few feet and vomited. The taxis I hailed wouldn't stop. I limped home, where the face in my mirror was ashen, the scalp black and crusted, one eye swollen shut.

Peter let himself in as grey light was seeping into the room. He had a bloody nose and bruises on his face. He looked at my wounds and said nothing, just ran water into the sink. I may not be around, he said, the next time, and left red streaks on my towels. Changing his shirt he let himself out again, and I fell asleep in bright sunshine to the sound of whistling in the street.

Lucy's journey is taking longer than expected. She and the dog have crossed deserts, forded rivers, hacked through jungle, scaled cliffs and plunged into valleys until they are quite dizzy. Now they are climbing a mountain pass where the wind is bitter and the snow knee-deep. Lucy's cloak is threadbare and she sleeps with her arms round the dog. Their food ran out two days ago. In late afternoon, as the sun turns the peaks a golden pink, she stops in the middle of a snowfield and sinks to the ground. I am weak with hunger, she says to the dog, I can go no further.

I am alarmed at the turn the story has taken. I scan the snowfield anxiously for signs of life. The dog licks Lucy's face and then bounds away over the snow. Where on earth is it going? Tasha! Tasha! calls Lucy, Come back! But Tasha has disappeared over the horizon. Lucy looks at the setting sun and the desolate snowfield and bursts into tears. How can the dog have abandoned her? There is not a house or a plume of smoke in sight. No food, no shelter, night falling.... Lucy's mother will never forgive me. Tasha, I shout, Tasha!

There is a noise at my side. I look up. The man from the gatehouse is standing there, hugging himself with his thin arms, his chin sunk in his chest. He smells sour and old in his ragged pants and bare feet. What has brought him out of his burrow? Doesn't he know that Lucy is freezing to death on the other side of the world? I thrust one of the almond cakes I brought for Lucy at him. He takes it, licks it cautiously, then clutches it to his chest and shuffles away.

I try to concentrate but darkness has fallen on the snowfield and I cannot see Lucy at all. And Tasha, where is Tasha? The only sound is the howling of the wind. I walk home slowly, stopping every few minutes, straining to hear.

Peter and I met now in deserted parking lots, abandoned buildings, behind boxcars at the freight-yard. It was no longer safe, he said, either at the café or my pension. I took a room I couldn't afford in a luxury hotel with security guards, but still he wouldn't come. Of course I love you, he said, but it isn't good for business. Klaus laughed when I told him. In this climate love needs fertilizing, he said, and rubbed his fingers together. He's found a wealthier gardener. Or a younger.

Klaus brought others to the café now who tossed their heads and flared their nostrils like Arabian colts, who drank our wine and fingered his blond hair. I spoke to them in their language and watched my words leap ravines, only to fall short. Sometimes I took one of them to the hotel, but there were no shutters, no pouting lips, no concealed doorways. When they left I wandered down to the docks where the fishermen mended their blue nets and the stevedores lifted crates onto glistening shoulders. I gorged myself on images of Peter smiling, teasing, looking at me from beneath his lashes, and grew pale and thin on my new diet.

Once we met in an old bunker on a hill outside the town. A rusting cannon faced an invisible enemy; people had carved their initials in the stone walls. I ran my fingers under his shirt and loosened his belt, but all I saw were soldiers with whips and jackboots. Peter complained that the earth floor was cold and hard. We heard distant voices coming up the hillside and got to our feet. For the first time Peter held out his hand. Don't follow me, he said, after I'd laid what bills I had on his palm, and when a couple and their children arrived I pretended, like them, to be just another tourist deciphering ancient messages of love.

I wake in the middle of the night out of a disturbed sleep. Tasha is bounding back over the horizon, bringing – I strain to see through the whirling snowflakes. I can just make out a tall figure in a hooded robe. I pull on my wine-stained pants and hurry down the street. I fumble with the chain at the entrance. There is the soft pad of paws, the brush of fur against my leg. I know my way even in the dark. My fingers touch the stone cherub, the stump of arm. I sit down, my heart beating. Hold on, Lucy, I say, help is coming. Tasha is bounding ahead through the snow, stopping now and then to check that the figure is still following. She reaches Lucy's inert body and begins to lick her face. The figure raises its staff and throws back its hood, looking remarkably like the man in the gatehouse. The staff glows like a band of sunlight; the snow melts; flowers spring from the ground. Lucy stirs suddenly and yawns and sits up. The staff glows again and a feast of honey cakes and fruit and wine appears. This is delicious, says Lucy, cramming fruit and cake into her mouth at the same time. You wouldn't happen to know where the jewelled palace is, would you?

Ah Lucy, answers do not come so easily, even in fairy-tales! But thank God she is alive and well. Perhaps things will turn out all right after all. I sag against the headstone.

Kill him, said the Moroccans. Defend your honour. We can arrange. They smiled and flicked their fingers at imaginary dust. I heard the husky voice cry out, saw the beautiful neck arch as it snapped in two.

I sold my father's books and Peter's necklace, I moved out of the hotel into a forgotten street. I sat in the café, unshaven, cuffs greasy, listening to the sounds of Moroccan and German under a brassy and distorting sun. I lifted my glass to my lips and set it down again like one of those figures in a circus booth with a slot for coins. How many raisings and lowerings were there, I wondered, between now and death? I would become a student of arm movements, elbow angles, minute alterations of finger position.

Klaus went away, travelling. The colts tossed their heads and went in search of new meadows. The Moroccans were summoned home by wives, sick relatives, visa difficulties. I sat with my glass, raising and lowering, wooden and deaf. Once I looked up and saw a boy who might have been Peter walking on the other side of the street. He was with someone, an older man, a foreigner. The man patted his cheek playfully; the boy turned and smiled. I raised my glass and two tiny misshapen figures appeared in its bowl.

Klaus did not return. The café owner sold up and went away. I raised and lowered my glass in a room without windows where there was nothing to distract me from my investigations.

Just a moonrise and a sunset away, says the old man, startling me. So Lucy's question will be answered after all! Just a moonrise and a sunset away, at the top of the crystal mountain, and you will find the palace. Thank you, says Lucy, and gathers up the remains of the feast in her kerchief. She sets off with Tasha, and when I look again the old man has vanished. In no time at all they are at the edge of the snowfield, looking at a glittering mountain in the distance with a tiny golden cube at the top. They cross the valley by moonlight and by sunset they are climbing the glass stairs that lead to the ruby doors.

A trumpet sounds and the huge doors open slowly. A young prince in gold brocade is coming down the stairs to greet them. He has white teeth and walnut skin and lashes like curtains. He takes Lucy by the hand and leads her into the palace, where all the courtiers bow low. Here is the lady of many journeys, he says, soon to be the princess of unexpected arrivals.

Just a minute, I want to say, Lucy belongs here with the stone cherub and the mossy headstone, but Lucy is already opening cupboards and inspecting the furniture. It's nice and warm, she says, looking round, and there's sure to be lots to eat. I must go home at once and tell my mother, she'll be worrying about me.

We'll send a carriage and six white horses for your mother, says the prince, and in the meantime we'll invite all the neighbouring kingdoms to a great feast. Lucy claps her hands and Tasha cavorts like a puppy, but I am regretting that I ever heard of a jewelled palace. Won't you miss the smell of earth, Lucy, the cherub's cold flesh, the roots of flowers tickling your feet? Won't you miss my visits, my almond cakes, my stories? But Lucy has disappeared and the ruby doors are beginning to swing shut.

I look round for the man in the gatehouse but he is nowhere in sight. I shut my eyes, I dig my fingers in the earth, I resist the closing of those doors with all the strength of my failing muscles. Yellow spots dance in front of my face. I hear the rasp of hinges, the turning of a great key, and when I look again the palace has faded and I meet the blind eyes of the cherub.

Lucy! Lucy!

We shall have a feast, Lucy, you and I. I will bring cheese and dates and olives, and we will sit here beside the mossy headstone while I tell a story about a boy with a scar under his heart. The old dog will lie down beside us, the man in the gatehouse will come, may even be bold enough to tell a story of his own. The shadows will lengthen, the angels take flight, and all of us, the living and the dead, will listen for the sound of voices behind shutters on an airless street.

ICE PALACE

IN THE SAME MONTH that ninety thousand men died in the mud at Ypres, Stefan Czerwinski stepped from a train into the shadow of the Rockies, wrists bound behind him. Stumbled down the embankment after the lieutenant's lantern, bareheaded in the lash of rain. Along a ragged trail marched between a Hungarian and a Czech whose moustache had trembled all the way from Calgary, a stump or deadfall leaping at them in the light. In two years in the coal mines near Jasper, on the railway at Yale, he had shattered an arm, three fingers, and a kneecap, had watched his brother's misshapen body pulled from a thousand tons of rock after the dynamite accident at Mile 41. Now, water seeping through his soles, he walked just in front of a private in khaki and puttees, the faint sheen of barbed wire somewhere ahead in the darkness.

Three years earlier he and Józef had stumbled from the S.S. *Ionian* onto the wharf at Halifax, mouths open, clutching suitcases tied with string. A week later lifted picks above the hard rocks of the New World, golden prairie still unrolling in their heads, the strange consonants making their jaws ache. After the accident, the fountain of rock that leapt a hundred feet in the air a present for Stefan's nineteenth birthday, he moved his arms faster, burying Józef again and again under the granite and basalt. Until he was sent reeling into the streets, holding his last pay packet, by the bullet that lodged in an archduke's breastbone in Sarajevo, the walls full of enlistment posters and the papers hissing of Prussian agitators, alien curs. The long blue shadows of the police, whispered a man from the neighbouring village of Jarosław, fell across anyone without work or papers. For nine months he hid: haylofts, abandoned buildings, the edges of bush. Stole chickens and potatoes, set snares for birds, flushed ground squirrels from their burrows with smoke. When the flashlight fell on his face one night in an empty barn near Pincher Creek it was almost a relief. For a week he sat in the jail's single cell, trading jokes and cigarettes with the constable, until they took him to the train station and turned him over to the 103rd Calgary Rifles.

Each day they were summoned from bed by the bugler at six. Shaved in tin basins outside under the chill hand of the mountains, ate thin porridge in rows on wooden benches, 491 spoons a drumbeat on metal plates. At six-thirty sharp assembled at the stockade gate and fell out into work gangs, Stefan and nineteen others marching between Ptes. O'Reilly and Thacker to the Camp Road worksite where they cleared brush, axes swinging in their thickened hands, mosquitoes circling their heads like moons round a planet. At noon bread and, if they were lucky, a bit of sausage, eaten leaning on their axe-handles, cigarettes cupped in their palms and flicked into the trees until seven men escaped under cover of a brush fire and smoking was forbidden. Then the long afternoons, the rising and falling again of the axes, Stefan pausing only to watch a young elk with its mossy rack until Pte. Thacker shouted. At five-thirty the march back to camp through Indian paintbrush and grass-of-Parnassus for dinner: 4 oz. potatoes, 2 oz. beans, 2 oz. pickled cabbage. In the evenings, under mountains wounded by late sun, the trading of hoarded spoonfuls of coffee, letters striped black with the censor's pencil, newspapers where Stefan followed events on the Eastern Front above a Ukrainian's squat finger, stumbling in and out of thickets of language. And in a quiet corner the delivery of coins and tightly folded bills to Kraszewski, his tripe-coloured face hanging above a guttering candle, Kraszewski who stood beside Major Stewart after church parade Sunday mornings and whose shameful mouth uttered the weekly penalties in German, Ukrainian, Polish.

Nights Stefan slept between an Austrian and a Croat, neither of whose dreams he understood when words poured out of their throats in the darkness. When he himself walked again down the wheel-rutted streets of Radymno, geese scattering and his mother running towards him, apron flying, calling *Stefek! Stefanek!* His father holding handfuls of turnips, smiling with his hoe over his shoulder, and his brothers butchering a pig for dinner, Józef in his new suit with the dirt from the coffin still clinging to the sleeves.

On Saturday afternoons Mrs. Stewart presided at tea in her tent in the officers' quarters. Parties of ladies motored up from town, accompanied by gentlemen in cravats and waistcoats who peered at the prisoners through Lieutenant Hay's field-glasses. Afterwards they were taken on a tour of the mess, the cookhouse, the jail. Stefan, at the edge of the group pressed to the barbed wire, watched the tulip dresses, the white-gloved hands, the hats nodding over the teacups. Turned his face away to escape the sweep of the lens. In the night he woke, vomiting up the watery beans, woke again in the dim afternoon orange of the hospital tent, temperature 104 degrees and tonsils like beetroot. Two of the tulip dresses stood at his bedside. One of them, dark hair escaping from a white veiled hat and a tiny mole above her upper lip, placed a Bible and a bag of sugared sweets in his hands. After they left he lifted the Bible to his face, the faint scent of her mixed with the sharp smell of uncut pages. In the morning, his fever broken, he remembered a dream of dark hair and white shoulders, fleshless until he saw the book on the bedside table.

In the village they said, All you get from life is a shirt with new buttons and a fistful of dirt. Was that all there was, the dim slipping past of years, the rows of turnips, a glass of *piwo* at the end of the day? One Christmas the youngest son of Stefan's next-door neighbour came back across the ocean wearing shoes you could see your face in, a watch fob hung with gems. Over there even the pigs smell sweeter, he said, dropping coins with a president's face on them into Stefan's palm. Stefan's brothers stood at a distance, spitting into the muddy street, but Stefan saw scented handkerchiefs, gilt doorknockers, women with fragile ankles. When the emigration agents came with their starched cuffs, their crisp contracts, he pushed Józef to the head of the line, the coins in his fist bearing the sweat of twelve different palms. A month later left for the border at Wesoła, he and Józef walking for two weeks at night, hiding by day, watching always for the blue uniforms of the Austrian soldiers. Eating, when their bread and cheese ran out, mushrooms and last year's rotted acorns.

He traded his canteen tickets for coins and stood in front of Kraszewski one evening. In my village, said Kraszewski, holding a coin to the light, we say the longer the goose's neck, the sooner it gets chopped off. Stefan added another coin to the pile. All I want is her name, he said. Three days later, after evening roll call, Kraszewski pressed his face against Stefan's ear. Elizabeth – the name melted like a sweet pretzel, even in Kraszewski's mouth! – Elizabeth Spence, age twenty-one, married with a nine-month-old child, only daughter of F. Irwin & Sons, provisioners to the camp. Husband Capt. Charles Spence, stationed overseas with the 48th Battalion of the Canadian Expeditionary Force. Kraszewski wiped his mouth and spat, told Stefan for another fifty cents he'd find a way to get a letter delivered.

Dark hair she unpinned at night, a husband in khaki who wrote letters from the front, a cradle with an embroidered coverlet she rocked in the evening lamplight. Stefan spent a week with an English dictionary and several sheets of paper, forcing fragrant visions into indigestible lumps.

Kindest madam,
I am difficult to speak in english what is in heart. You look like angel beside bed. I am very much care for holy Book. Can you please writing a letter soon! I see you are most kind person.

Stefan Czerwinski
Prison camp

On September 15th the first snow fell.

Each night Stefan stepped from a lighted train into a dark forest, a rifle barrel in the small of his back. Sometimes the train was moving and he had to jump, only to see his father waving to him from a window as the train gathered speed. Other nights he was with Józef, Józef who lifted his bound hands and begged Stefan to release him. On the worst nights there was no train and no rifle; he was by himself climbing a dark mountain towards a light that kept getting fainter and higher. He carried picks and shovels, his pockets were full of stones, and from somewhere came the sound of screaming.

He slept now in his clothing, woke still shivering under the thin blanket, snapped ice from the tin basin for a shaving mirror. Major Stewart ordered his own heater placed in the prisoners' sleeping quarters and wrote, again, to the commanding officer of Military District 13 requesting additional boots and mackinaws. In the third week of September five more prisoners escaped. Prisoner No. 109, Jelinek, J., was recaptured three miles downriver and sentenced to fourteen days' solitary confinement.

Stefan waited two weeks, then late one evening pushed Kraszewski into the slops at the back of the cookhouse and held him down with his boot. The letter – Kraszewski heaved and struggled – had been posted that same day by Major Stewart's batman. Was it his fault if the lady was offended by the droolings of an unlettered polack? Stefan lifted his boot and Kraszewski swore, brushed mouldy scraps from his shoulders.

He sent another letter, at double the cost.

Snow lining their collars, they marched four miles each morning to the quarry across from the great hotel above the falls, frozen in mid-leap. Deaf from the noise of the rock crusher, moustache glazed with ice, Stefan no longer felt the pick handle between his numb hands. When the fuses were lit, pieces of rock falling out of the sky, he saw his brother's face, the flesh peeled back along the arms. At lunch they stood back to back for warmth, breath rising like cattle's, watching the tiny figures on the hotel's stone ramparts, its copper roof glinting with frost. Once he thought he saw her, hands in a white fur muff, looking over the railing at the spray of ice far below. Hadn't she understood his letters? Was she angry that he'd dared to write? When Olinyk the joker waved his frozen bread at the hotel and shouted, Under a fur coat a naked ass like yours and mine! Pte. Jermyn cut the laughter by sending them back to work eleven minutes early.

In November Prisoner No. 57, Kavčič, H., was shot through

the neck and buttocks attempting to escape from a woodcutting party a mile northeast of camp. Two weeks later Ptes. Thacker and Desmond were court-martialled for allowing five prisoners to escape during the dinner hour. One of these, a boy from a village eight miles from Stefan's own, was discovered by Kraszewski hiding in the quartermaster's tent and handed over to the guards. Major Stewart sent for Stefan, shoulders square under his jacket, his swagger stick gleaming on the desk between them. The boy spoke no English and Kraszewski didn't understand his dialect. Would Stefan translate at the hearing?

No.

Wolves shaped from snow, a rink lit with torches, a palace of ice for the King himself – at least, so one of the Hungarians had been told by the grocer's delivery boy. In town men strung red, white, and blue bunting between lampposts, carpenters hammered nails into a viewing platform outside the town hall. Stefan, marched with twenty other trouble-makers in lightly falling snow down Main Street, saw only the stares, the averted faces, the small crowds of boys, pointing. Bent his back among the tumbled blocks of ice as high as a man's waist, leaning into the rope between Olinyk and Pavic, faces pressed together like lovers.

Surely the grave face that looked out at them from the green penny stamps would bend to listen, order the stockade gates opened wide! Taking no chances, the Ukrainians had borrowed Stefan's dictionary and drafted a petition. After the Austrians tore it up and bloodied several Ukrainian noses, Stefan heard his own name read out among the Melnyczuks and Uhlmanns on the morning's charge sheet, sent to lift and pull and sweat under the gaze of well-fed faces.

At his heels a thousand pounds of ice ground over the street, spray rising above his head like smoke, his boots slipping on packed snow. Yards away the whip curling over the horses pulling the sleds, manes clotted with frost. Turning, he saw battlements of crystal fifty feet in the air, turrets at each corner you could see the sky through, clear as glass. Blinded by the glare, stomach hollow, he stepped forward to touch, hands swimming through air. Woke staring at the clouds, Olinyk unknotting him from the rope.

That fall the Eleventh German Army swept across the Vistula, a path of flame thirty miles wide springing from their heels as they marched east. Stefan no longer stepped from a lighted train; he saw thatched roofs burning, riderless horses, a woman running down a street with her arms empty. The District Officer Commanding arrived in a black staff car in late November to inspect the troops. Major Stewart, announcing the formation of a clean-up party, stood alone; Kraszewski, so a Bulgarian whispered, had been caught stealing strawberry jam from the officers' mess.

Under the kerosene lamp that evening the major tapped two soiled blue envelopes against his knuckles, Stefan watching the light on the regimental cufflink. Is this your writing, Czerwinski? Kraszewski, who had pulled Stefan, in shaving brush moustache, from a knot of laughing Czechs, stood in a corner wiping his nose with a handkerchief. You realize, of course, that posting uncensored letters is a flagrant breach of wartime regulations. Not to mention bribery and threatening a fellow prisoner. Kraszewski coughed; Stefan lifted his chin and stared through the tent wall at the cobbled square of Kraków where over a hundred years ago the great Kościuszko had sworn his oath of defiance against three kingdoms. If you have nothing to say I shall order you assigned extra duties until further notice. I won't demean myself by reading your impertinent remarks to the lady in question. As Kraszewski stepped forward to lead Stefan out of the tent Major Stewart struck a match and fed the envelopes into the flame.

The Slovaks spoke of the border three hundred miles south beyond which there was no barbed wire, no angry bayonets, all the sausage you could eat. The Croats of the passes west through the mountains, the safe houses on the other side where you were passed hand to hand like a parcel on your way to the coast. The Ukrainians, piecing together the petition, of the young prince who was coming instead of his father, the one who had offered his castle for quartering troops and had danced with commoners in London clubs before the war. In the darkness, holding the Bible, Stefan moved his lips: Holy Mary, Queen of Poland, keep her safe, remind her of a man she touched once who speaks to her in dreams.

In the evenings they practised standing at attention and bowing when their names were called; a Croat who'd lived briefly in England assured them the English did not kiss each other on the hand. The Ukrainians borrowed Stefan's dictionary again and whispered in corners. Marching back to camp in the evenings they saw Indian tepees rising in the centre of the street, frozen elk springing from blocks of ice, men in muskrat parkas hurrying past with chisels, lamps, shovels.

In the village were they waiting for the Messiah, rising at dawn to light single candles in the church? His mother preparing fragrant *barszcz*, spicy *piernik*, the unleavened wafers of the Christ Child tucked under a white cloth in a basket, ready to be handed round the table when the evening star rose. Stefan unpacked cabbages in the cookhouse, lifting them from their nest of newspapers. Tracing a headline with his mittened finger: *Mayor Chisholm to Welcome Duke and Duchess of Devonshire*. Repeating aloud the words he didn't know, watching their shapes in the cold air so he could look them up later. *Royal Highnesses. Gladdening the hearts of Canadians at this sombre time. Distinguished guests at the Winter Festival Ball*. Above the cabbages he saw Elizabeth, in sequins and white gloves, curtseying before the duke under the chandeliers, then whirling away on his arm as the violinists danced their bows across the strings. Elizabeth, who had read not one of his slow uncertain words, who did not remember a man who had tossed under her hand in an orange tent. Who tilted her head, instead, to gilt epaulettes, a chestful of medals, a trim beard. Later, a small crowd leaning round his cot, he described the duke with his ceremonial sabre, the duchess enfolded in fur, the orchestra coming all the way from Edmonton, the dinner of venison, pheasant, cherries jubilee.

He stood with Olinyk and Balacz on top of the south wall, levering a turret block into place with rope, ten men staggering underneath as it rose into the air. The hair in their nostrils freezing, eyelashes stuck together, Stefan remembering a dead cow he'd seen once crumpled on its knees, tongue frozen to an iron gate. Translucent Walls a Thing of Beauty, said the paper, noting that several worthy citizens had turned out, at thirty-five below, to assist on the last tower, fortified with hot chocolate and buttered rum from a nearby hotel-keeper.

On the feast of the Immaculate Conception Prisoner No. 57, Kavčič, H., died of his wounds, his body sent under guard to the morgue in Calgary. The Slovenes held an impromptu memorial service, kneeling round a candle on the dirt floor, reciting long mouthfuls of prayer, throaty and harsh. Stefan heard them, a distant singing, through the walls of the cook-house in the pauses between lifting tubs of lard. To die where no one remembered your village, your father, your grand-father, to die without the blessing of the priest, the paleness of the women's faces under their kerchiefs. One's own language chewed, swallowed, ploughed under like last year's stubble. Even for Józef there'd been a mass said by a young priest who'd left the old country with his parents twenty years before. Stefan flung one of the tubs against the wall so hard the staves split, the white fat oozing over his boots.

Twenty men with drums and bagpipes marked time in front of the viewing platform, plaid ribbons snapping in the wind. Stefan stood with the cold breath of the wall at his back, knees bruised from scaling it that afternoon to plant the British flag he'd strapped to his body. Beside him Olinyk, gold tooth winking, crackle of paper under his coat when he shifted position. Fifty of them, freshly shaved, would hold out one hand after another from ragged cuffs, reaching across barbed wire and centuries to a king's ambassador. Hems of sheared beaver and otter brushing their legs now as the crowd moved forward, mouthing O's at the shining battlements, the coloured lights.

A hundred yards away a black car paused, its door swung wide by a young private, and the man in the photograph climbed out, top hat in hand. Behind him a woman with foxtails at her throat, hand fluttering in the air, ankles Stefan could have circled between finger and thumb. The bagpipes swelling as a thousand tiny flags quivered, an honour guard presented arms, gold and silver stars burst above the roof of the town hall. Major Stewart stepped forward, flanked by two officers, the duke inclining his narrow face with its little beard.

Here he was, this man of noble blood whose hand would be offered that evening to a woman with a tiny mole on her upper lip. Walking towards them, his wife beside him, the major pointing with his swagger stick to the turrets that rose into the sky. Stefan saw a full mouth, a fair complexion, a nervous habit of lifting an eyebrow. Pulling off his cap saw him reach out a gloved hand to Balacz, then Danyluk, felt the slender fingers grasp his own for a moment under some murmured phrase he didn't catch. The duchess held out gold-ringed fingers bluish with cold. Stefan dropped to his knees, pressing his lips against perfumed softness, turning the tender palm against his face. The hand curling and pulling away so that he had to hold it more tightly, force open the fingers even as he heard her cry out and felt his arms seized. He struggled to hold the fluttering hand but it broke free and flew to her mouth, her face a white oval floating in the darkness as he was dragged away across the snow.

FINN SLOUGH

EVENINGS AFTER my paper route I rode home along the river, stopping to pick early blackberries in the ditch. Cars drove past me in the dusk, gleam of sunset on chrome, people's heads tipped back, drinking. I knelt in the mud where the berries grew thickest, the brambles catching my inky hands. Once I'd seen the blue-eyed boy who sat behind me in physics driving with the new girl who lived three streets over. I'd bent over my bicycle, pretending to tighten the rusted spokes.

We lived in a brown house on a blind street my father had walked down years ago, not looking back. My mother would be waiting, plates heating in the oven, stray hairs damp at her temples. I swung onto my bicycle, moths brushing my face, the sky bright with projector beams and words whispering up at me out of the bushes: promise, forever, love, kiss. Kisses and whispers and that pink and silver glow above me in the sky, a thousand faces tilted upwards. At graduation the week before I'd watched one of the lawyers' sons throw up over my new white heels. I'd spat out the cherry wine spiked with vodka, run home in my stockinged feet.

My last summer of freedom, so my mother said. Already I fed the babies of the woman next door, wiped tables at a coffee shop Saturdays, but at the end of summer I had to find a job. You'll get to wear seamed nylons and a good tweed skirt, said my mother, vacuuming the living room floor. I saw myself with my hair pinned up, moving papers around on a desk, my pencil running in tiny squiggles over a notebook under a man's furrowed gaze. Was that what my life would be, tiny squiggles all the way to the horizon? I thought of the words whispering out of the bushes, the glow in the sky, that distant shimmer in the heavens.

On an airless afternoon my mother cashed in a savings bond and took me to try on suits. In the sticky dimness of the shop I tried on navy suits, herringbone, double-breasted, plain, while my mother frowned, tilted her head, made me walk up and down. The saleswoman brought belts, brooches, scarves. As I stood in front of the full length mirror they poked and patted and tucked and pulled. The rack of discards outside the changing room grew. Is there nothing else? said my mother.

From a back corner the saleswoman brought a light grey worsted with white piping round the lapels. The sleeves were too long and the skirt hung on my narrow hips, but my mother and the saleswoman both smiled. Won't you look smart at your interviews! said the saleswoman, pinching a seam. Come in for a fitting on Monday. I saw a row of us in white piping, fingers flying above typewriters, notepads, files.

I arrived just before closing, breathless, my bag of papers empty, my fingers ink-stained. A young woman in a blue smock came out of the stock room, pins in her mouth and a tape measure curling round her neck. Hold out your arm, she said. Bracelets jangled as she took my wrist between plump fingers and ran the tape to my armpit. When she knelt to measure my hem length I saw a pale brown birthmark at the nape of her neck. Her long black hair brushed my knee. My fingers tingled, my knuckles turned to water. Narrow bones and long feet, she said, standing up, the legs of a dancer. You don't dance? The smell of sweat and floor polish, vomit, cherry wine rose about me. A young girl like you, should be out dancing all the time! She snapped her fingers and spun in front of me, her tape measure spreading like a shawl. A saleswoman called from the depths of the store: Radojka!

I see you on Friday for first fitting, she said, tossing my suit over her shoulder. The *Lilengro*, Finn Slough. As she walked away her thimble spun upwards like a top and disappeared.

Radojka. I sat upright in bed, half asleep, seeing again the first day of school last September, the young woman in the torn skirt, the black hair. She stood at the front of the class in bare feet, holding a battered pencil case. Bet she's off one of the farms in the valley, went the whisper up and down the rows of desks. Behind her back they called her Radish, mimicked her accent, said gypsy dago jew. She walked alone up the polished corridors on her way to the next class, her bracelets jangling, looking neither to right nor left. On the second day she wasn't there. I found the pencil case in her empty locker and a piece of what looked like leather, brown and shrivelled. I kept them for her, but she didn't return.

My mother was silent at breakfast, stirring the eggs round on her plate. The corner of a blue envelope stared from under her napkin. When will that suit be ready? she said after my brother had gone out to play. And don't run off when you've finished, I have to go to town.

I saw her in hat and gloves in the post office, counting out crumpled bills across the counter, writing an address in her upright hand. The blue envelope added to the stack in her bottom drawer, sent from towns that zigzagged across the continent. You don't have to answer him, I said.

She put down her cup and dabbed at her mouth. That wouldn't be Christian. He might be ill. Or dying.

Lying in a gutter, more likely, I said. She flung down her napkin and slapped me, hard, across the cheek, then ran from the room.

I stared in the bathroom mirror at the mark, the fingerprints mottling in the tan of my cheek.

Ducks rose, squawking, as I walked my bike past the marsh grass at the edge of the slough, past the *Sarah Maria*, the *Breezy Lady*, their paint peeling, decks awash in flowers. Gin Slough, people called it, where drunks went, criminals, where a child had been murdered once, long ago. The *Lilengro* had a leaning chimney, nasturtiums in window-boxes, a black cat with white paws perched on the life preserver. Several little girls skipping rope on the deck stopped to stare at me. I leaned my bike against the starboard bow. The door swells up in hot weather, Radojka shouted when I knocked. You pull while I push. I seized the knob, tugged, and Radojka tumbled out almost on top of me while the cat hissed and fled.

In the sudden darkness of the galley kitchen Radojka poured me a glass of wine, hunted under the table for pins and scissors. She pulled the suit from a pile in a corner and held it against me, lips puckering. Makes you look like old woman. Put it on. I turned my back, slid my jeans off under the skirt. Radojka gave me the pincushion to hold and knelt beside me, pulling at the basting thread. A pouch on a thong at her neck swung against my leg. I remembered the shrivelled leather in my night-table drawer. That stuff you left behind at school? I said. I kept it for you.

Radojka grabbed my arm, scattering pins. I spat curses over that, I wished them all ill, she said. You must go home at once and throw away. Over your shoulder, without looking. Come back tomorrow for your suit.

I rode home with the smell of wine and slough air on my skin, the sky darkening to rain. My mother was waiting, drumming her fingers on the screen door. After supper she sat at the kitchen table, her pencil darting over the classifieds, while I took the scrap of leather outside and burned it in a barrel, the flames singeing my face.

Why was I drawn to her? Perhaps because I was crooked too, broke mirrors when I looked in them and memorized the dictionary backwards, or so they said each year when I won the annual spelling bee. My hair hung limp and straight, not bouffant blonde like the other girls, and my chest was as flat as a boy's. The others bled, I knew, every month, but though I inserted pencils, rulers, even the poker, no blood came. I was seventeen and becalmed, my body hairless, unyielding.

When I came up the gangplank Radojka was sitting at the table sewing tiny stitches across a cloud of white lace. For the daughter of an important lady, she said, holding up a long white dress. A big August wedding. I show you. She slipped off her skirt and blouse and stood there naked, thick curls sprouting between her legs. When she pulled the dress over her head and shook out the skirt it fitted her perfectly. She twirled in the narrow space between cupboards, said she would marry too someday, maybe the doctor's boy who came to the boat Friday nights or the principal's son who came Saturdays. In a dress of multicoloured velvet, she said, with a bouquet of

swamp nettles and burdock, the ring under the minister's eyes
a wriggling catfish, leaping off the cushion and slithering
among the guests.

She took out a glass and the wine bottle as I put on the suit,
freshly ironed. The narrowed jacket added curves to my chest,
flared over my narrow hips. Radojka brushed tailor's chalk
from the lapels. I sewed heron feathers and rosemary in the
lining for luck, she said. *Kooshto bok!* She drained the glass,
wiped the rim on her lacy skirt before giving it to me.

As I mounted my bike she handed me the suit, neatly
wrapped and tied with string. My mother wrinkled her nose as
she shook out the jacket and held it up. She examined Radojka's
tiny stitches, watched as I walked up and down the hallway. I'm
sure that kickpleat's higher, she said. Now remember to cross
your legs when you sit. There's the strangest smell in here, did
you notice? – and she went to open a window.

I went for an interview one hot day in a pillared temple on a
downtown street. I twisted my hair up in a French braid and
held still while my mother applied pink lipstick to my mouth.
She pulled a thread from my jacket, pressed coins in my
fingers, repeated the directions as I ran out the door.

Inside the building all sound had floated up to the high ceiling and vanished. Figures came and went between the brass
grilles at the counter and the long rows of desks. My hands
were clammy, my mouth dry. A woman with a pinched mouth
motioned me inside a doorway. Another woman sat there,
blonde hair skewered with combs, a jacket buttoned tight to
her neck.

You're applying for the job of ledger clerk? I can't hear you,
speak up. Do they teach you to add out there where you live?
Here's some figures, you've got three minutes.

The numbers wriggled and danced before my eyes, little
minnows. I didn't get the job. So she thinks we live in the
sticks, does she? said my mother, stabbing my brother's shirt
with the iron. You'd better practise adding before your next
interview. And look at me when I'm talking to you.

At night I saw each figure clear and steady on the white
paper, added the column up, down and sideways, tossed the

numbers in the air and caught them in my teeth. I dispensed crisp handfuls of them, snapping like biscuits, to a long lineup of people standing at my grille: Radojka, the blue-eyed boy, my mother, even the groaning lawyer's son. At the end of the day I pulled down a little screen at my station and walked out, my footsteps ringing in the vaulted air.

Along Finn Slough at dusk the water oily with light, Radojka chopping onions at the stove as the little girls ran in and out carrying the one-eyed kitten. Motioning at a stool with her knife, feeding me bread and wild strawberry jam while she talked. Of travels in a country where the wolves still howled and you could snap pieces of sky off like icicles, of desert towns where women slid between the houses like scorpions and the date palms cast no shadows. I stirred the jam with my finger and told her about the notebook squiggles. She fed her sisters chicken soup flavoured with nettles, shooed them to bed, brushed crumbs from the table. Drew out the cards, kissed the deck, and laid out the Devil, the Magician, the Hermit, the Fool. You are in a ballroom, she said. You are wearing sapphires, everyone's eyes are on you. And there is a man standing near you – I cannot see his face – She turned a card over. Ah, now the scene has changed. You are standing on golden sand by a distant ocean. And there is a boy coming towards you, a boy with blue eyes.... Yellow spots formed in front of my face, the air felt thick as cotton. This boy, said Radojka, you know him already? Silence, in which even the clock didn't tick, the tap stopped dripping. Radojka gathered up the cards, straightened them with her strong brown fingers. You must go, I will be busy. Come on Monday and bring me an empty jar, with a lid.

As I wheeled my bike away I could see her through the window, the knife in her hand throwing sparks as she held the blade to the whetstone.

Finn Slough? said my mother at dinner one night. You've been going to Finn Slough? Perhaps it was the bracelet of river water that gave me away, the look on my face, the smell of my hair. My mother caught my hand and tilted my chin up. You are not, I repeat *not*, to go there. My brother snickered. And you, you can help your sister with the dishes after.

Boats and the smell of onions, the snap of cards and the glitter of oily water at dusk. My mother's face, the table, the yellow tablecloth grew wavery and distant like heat rising on a road. In my room I pulled the covers over my head and felt the floor tilt, felt the slap and rock of water, heard Radojka bend over me and murmur words in an unknown language.

I heard my mother calling as I ran out of the yard with the jar hidden in my paper bag. I leapt on my bike and pedalled hard, head down. In three hours I had to walk through a door where a man in a stiff collar sat tapping a pencil on his desk. This time I'd add up figures so fast I'd make him dizzy.

Radojka was standing on the deck stirring something in a large kettle, her apron flapping. Hurry! she called. Bring me the jug from the fridge. I carried a pitcher containing some milky liquid out onto the deck. Pour it slowly into the pot while I stir, she said. And close your eyes. I smelt seawater and pine needles, dried blood, rotting fungus. I saw rows of desks, the blond nape just in front of me, so close I could have reached out and touched it. The classroom disappeared and he stood there before me, blue-eyed, smiling, the nose slightly crooked.

Open your eyes, said Radojka. Something, a bone, a piece of gristle, bobbed there at the surface. I turned my head away while Radojka dipped a ladle into the kettle and held it out. I tasted salt, fruitcake, a meadowful of flowers. Radojka laughed. Fruitcake means a wedding, she said, salt is for luck. Another spoonful. This time it was spinach, cough medicine, sugar doughnuts. Many children and a long life, said Radojka. A most favourable sign.

She ladled the liquid, a pale clear amber, into the jar I held out. Keep it under your bed at night, take three tablespoons a day, she said. And then? I asked. We must wait and see, she said.

The kitchen clock said ten to six when I came in the door carrying the jar under my jacket. I shook my watch, which said one-fifteen. My newly ironed suit hung from one of the cupboard doors. My mother said nothing, drew a plate from the oven and set it on the table. For the first time I noticed the dark circles under her eyes. The fish in my mouth tasted like chalk, I couldn't eat.

Upstairs I placed the jar under my bed and summoned the blue-eyed boy, but I saw only my mother's face, then my father's, dimly remembered, then a man with a tight collar under his chin. The faces wavered, transparent, merged into one as I fell asleep.

I waited three days. In the mornings I felt my pulse, stuck out my tongue, examined the hidden places. I waited for my fingers to tingle, my hair to curl, my breasts to swell.

On the third night I climbed out of my bedroom window and ran, past the sleeping houses, the silvered river. As I knocked at the door of the *Lilengro*, shivering, I heard murmured voices, laughter. The door opened and Radojka stood there in her slip, a strap falling down, hair tumbled. What are you doing here, almost midnight? Wait there.

The door closed. I heard rustlings, Radojka's voice, another deeper one. The door opened again and a young man came out, buttoning his shirt. Radojka threw his shoes after him. I stared as Radojka pulled me inside, yawning. You are so impatient! Hold out your hands.

She bent over as I held them, palms up, under the dim lamp. There was a smell about her I didn't know, a salty smell like the slough itself.

You have been taking three tablespoons a day? You haven't missed? I shook my head. There should be a change, she said. It is hard to explain, a kind of glow under the skin…. She straightened, patted my shoulder. But your heart is like a green twig. It takes longer to catch when building a fire.

The blue-eyed boy who stood smiling on the deck took several steps backwards and vanished. My mother was right – as far as the eye could see were those tiny squiggles in a notebook. I stood up. What they said about you is true, I said. You're a liar and a witch. Radojka grabbed at my arm but I yanked open the door and ran. Perhaps she could change herself into a dog, a leopard, come leaping after me? I ran faster, the bushes a blur, my cheeks wet, until I saw the row of neat clipped houses in the moonlight. I stumbled up the path, my legs like rubber, climbed the drainpipe and eased myself over the sill. When I emptied the jar in the bathroom a cloud of steam rose, making me cough, and the porcelain was streaked with pink and silver like fish-scales. I rinsed and rinsed but it wouldn't come off. In the morning my mother said, Seems someone broke a bottle of nail-polish in the sink. You look exhausted, couldn't you sleep?

Just after the first heavy dews began I started work. I rode the bus each morning in my new suit, rode back each night. In between I added up long columns of figures that no longer hid in corners or scurried across the page. At the end of two weeks I held in my hand a piece of paper with numbers stamped on it in ridged blue lines. I bought chocolates for my mother and another suit, navy shantung with a silk carnation in the buttonhole. It slid off the rack onto my shoulders as though made for me. It's very becoming, dear, said my mother when I put it on the next morning. But you've lost weight. I was losing my summer tan too, and the band of river water round my wrists. At night Radojka walked in front of me up an endless corridor with polished floors. I ran after her but she turned a corner and disappeared. I searched room after room, opened cupboards, looked under desks, and found myself on an empty street filled with echoes under a grey sky.

At work now I typed letters and took them to be signed. They ordered a new desk for me, an upholstered chair. Two young men arrived with the furniture one morning. Lifted my old desk like a feather, pushed the new one into place. The dark-haired one pulled out an invoice for me to sign. Before sliding it into his pocket he looked at my name, said it out loud, smiled.

We went to a greasy spoon the next day for lunch. He ate a hamburger and fried onion rings, the muscles in his throat working as he swallowed, thick fingers tearing at the bread. That night we sat in his car and felt the patterns of light on our faces as the two enormous heads on the screen moved towards each other. He didn't talk but drew me to him across the seat, held me in the curve of his arm. Later, parked in the bushes by the river, he forced open my lips and kissed me. I'd never had a man's tongue in my mouth before, this fish thrashing its tail in my throat. I pulled away. First time? he said. I don't believe it. You look like you know how.

At home I held my hands to the light, looked in the mirror, stuck out my tongue. That glow Radojka had talked about, had it appeared after all? I touched my lips with my fingers. Something felt different. When I washed my hands the water ran pink and silver and the tidemark round my wrists wouldn't go away.

I bought chrysanthemums on my lunch break and set out after work, still in my suit and pumps. I smelled it first, the brackish air, the salty mud, and then I saw the peeling paint-work, the tilting chimney, the little girls playing hopscotch on the deck.

Radojka came to the door with her thimble on her finger, bits of thread clinging to her hair. Her face was pale, her mouth unsmiling. She shut the door in my face and yelled through it. Set foot in my house, she said, and your children will be three-toed and dull-witted.

I took a deep breath and told her about the dancing numbers, the polished corridor, the echoing sky. Also the new furniture, the greasy spoon, the fish in my throat. I laid the flowers on the windowsill and walked down the gangplank. When I reached the bottom she opened the door.

What colour is the water when you wash?

She told me to wait and shut the door again. I saw her through the window, burning candles and scattering petals. When she opened the door she held a dress in her arms, a blue silk dress with a bodice that shivered like water. I stepped into its folds; the silk rippled over my collarbone, the skirt floated around me. The room had turned wavery, I couldn't speak. Radojka took me by the hand and led me outside, the air cool on my skin. Swallows skimmed the surface of the slough. Humming, she put a hand at my waist, began moving her feet, while the breeze caught our dresses and blew the hair back from our faces.

ARABIAN SNOW

IN THE LITTLE SHOP with wheat-sheaves painted on the front door Gabriela plunged her fists into the bowl of dough, knocking its breath out. The baby slept at her feet, fingers curled round a bagel. Behind her on the bare brick wall one of Paul's paintings hung, a burnished charcoal like the welded steel of a ship. A Russian sailor had traded the painting for three loaves of her caraway rye bread, and how could she say no when he'd smiled at her like that through his gold teeth, tucked the warm loaves under his thin arms? His most treasured possession, this painting, produced by a famous Russian artist, a certain Pavel Petrovich, she could see his illegible scrawl in the bottom right corner. But one had to eat and the bread on his ship was worm-eaten, part wood shavings. An art dealer among her customers told her the painting had been cut from its frame and was probably stolen. She hung it anyway and began to notice a slight roll to the floor on windy days, when it was difficult to keep her footing carrying the pans. On one such day the wind blew a man with paint on his fingers into the shop, and while she guided a loaf through the slicer he cried out so that her hand almost slipped between the blades. The painting! Where had she got that painting? It had disappeared en route to a gallery in St. Petersburg, his first exhibition abroad, he'd never expected to see it again. Of course he had no alternative, once he'd heard the story, but to ask her to marry him. They waited six months while he built a studio over the shop, the odours of baking bread mingling with the tempera so that his paintings took on a yeasty quality as though they were alive, while customers bought loaves that made them smell salt air, breathe deeply, walk a little faster. And a year after that, on a tingling January morning, Gabriela's belly so round she couldn't get close enough to the bowl to knead, Minna tumbled through the frosty air into the doctor's outstretched and astonished hands, the soles of her blue feet crusted with salt.

Lucky Gabriela, everyone said. A beautiful baby, a talented husband, a little shop all her own where butter turns into coins. Life's wonderful, Gaby. Actually it wasn't, though the clock ticked, the ovens hummed, the espresso machine hissed softly to itself, though outside in a dawn breeze the cherry blossoms sifted to the ground like flour. Impossible to believe, looking at the growing baby, the rising dough, the floating blossoms, but the dreams had begun again.

Through the falling flakes I ride out of the grounds at Finsbrekken, my father's gyrfalcon perched on my wrist. My brothers are hunting deer, I can hear the dogs baying in the distance. The first snow has come early this year. My maid is packing the chests that will travel with me to the new country. Will he admire my bridal gown with its slashed sleeves, my grandmother's gilt circlet? I hear they sacrifice goats to the gods, keep their women under lock and key. The falcon jerks her hooded head at the sound of the dogs.

They'd begun in the hospital. On the second night, the baby asleep in the crib beside her, Gabriela woke with the sheets in her fists, the pillow damp with sweat. She'd been somewhere among sand dunes, palm trees, minarets, her face covered in a white veil. The sound of the muezzin's cry changed to the thin wail of the baby. Give birth to a child and you'll give birth to dreams, said the nurse who lifted Minna into her mother's arms. *My* mother, may God keep her in peace, dreamt of tigers and jungles. Gabriela smiled and bit her lip as Minna tugged at the nipple, as the smell of hot sand gave way to a scent of damp grass and milk.

In the morning Paul came with croissants and newspapers, yellow paint on his shirt, the smell of exhaust and the hum of traffic like a cloud around him. Walked up and down with his thumb in his daughter's fist calling her Minnow, little Minnow, teensy-weensy kootchy-wootchy Minnow, while Gabriela watched the wrinkled monkey face, the newborn rawness, as though she'd given birth to a shelled shrimp. Butter glazes called to her from the little shop, steam rising from new loaves, dough twisting like ribbon in her hands. In the

afternoon, drifting in and out of sleep, she walked through a
courtyard of turquoise tiles where a fountain sparkled in sunlight and a nightingale sang in a cage. That evening she asked
for a sleeping pill and sank dreamlessly onto a cloud of feathers until the rattle of the breakfast trays woke her.

Back home she laid the baby on a folded towel in one of the
larger baking pans and went on with her measuring, her stirring, her kneading, her face flushed in the glow from the
ovens. Rose at two to make corn and herb bread, date and walnut bread, golden baguettes, leaf-shaped *epis*, while upstairs
Paul painted another of his steel-eyed coyotes, its fur bristling
off the canvas. And also Irish soda bread, Finnish coffee bread,
Greek *kouloura*, Polish *babka*, while the city slept, the telephone wires hummed, a siren ki-iyed past like a wild animal.
In between batches she nursed Minna or changed diapers,
sprinkling flour on the baby's damp bottom, though once she
grabbed the cinnamon instead by mistake. What a wonderful
baby! everyone said. Slept through the night, smiled on sched-
ule, and was so quiet Gabriela kept misplacing her behind the
flour bins or under an orange crate. She was learning early that
ovens were hot, paint tasted awful, and the world smelled of
yeast, new canvas, and raisins – a perfect preparation, as Paul
said, for life. Fat toothless hairless Minnow, who had only to
wave her fists for some customer to melt like butter on warm
bread, but who was not nearly so beautiful as a row of rounded
loaves fresh from the oven.

The starlings were whistling in a peach sky when Gabriela
filled baskets with cinnamon buns, stacked loaves on shelves,
unlocked the door of the shop. Customers jostled and pushed,
drawn by the bread that made them hear paws in the forest,
raised the hair on the backs of their necks. Minna crawled
among tall and short, thin and fat legs, putting crumbs in her
mouth. At last the cash register fell silent, the shop door
closed, and Gabriela laid her head on the counter while Minna
sat sucking her thumb among the empty baking pans.

My father promised three pairs of gyrfalcons to the traders
when they came to Bergen in their djellabas, asking for the

master falconer to the king. When they came to Finsbrekken,
they saw me, and took a lock of blonde hair to the man who
had commissioned them. Now the falcons go as a wedding
gift and I travel with them, a lure they have caught.

What will I need in that strange new country? My squirrel
cape, except I am told I will faint from the heat. My willow
flute, but who will know our country dances? My small dog
Ratcatcher, though he may be eaten by jackals or poisoned by
snakes. I will take only my missal and crucifix, and ask for a
chapel to be built to Our Lady.

The sound of hooves ringing on ice woke her. Where was
she? She reached for the ball she'd been throwing for her small
dog and touched the blue quilt, the flowered sheets, the pine
night-table. Smelled the cherry blossom through the open
window and heard Paul laughing, Minna's shriek of pleasure.
The air changed, the bed righted itself, the small dog ran yap-
ping into the distance and disappeared.

At Paul's opening people wandered among the grey and blue
and yellow coyotes with their cheque-books open, little red
dots sprouting beside the paintings like measles. Gabriela
served cheese straws, seafood en croute, and even a pastry
shaped like a coyote's paw which had guests pouncing at each
other and snarling up and downstairs. Afterwards they drank
champagne out of Paul's shoe, linked arms with the gallery
owner, and visited all the bars between the east side and the
waterfront, Paul staggering finally along the edge of the wharf,
arms flapping above the oily water. Stumbling and falling as
Gabriela screamed. But catching himself on the hawser of a
huge ship, the name HALLINGSKARV lettered along its bow. As
the gallery owner pulled him to safety the ship's sails unfurled,
a flag bearing a crown flapped in the breeze, a sailor with a spy-
glass appeared in the crow's-nest. Gabriela tried to call out but
the wind rose, spray dashed against the hull, the wooden timbers creaked and shuddered. Sailors ran back and forth shouting, another scrambled up the rigging, a small white dog raced
along the deck. Gabriela's knees buckled. Out of the darkness
she heard someone calling, then fell into mist. In the morning

Paul teased her about too much champagne and remembered nothing, not even the strength of the rope that had saved him.

I had hoped we would be dashed to pieces in the storm, but we laid over for repairs at the Cape and disembarked at last in this land where the light burns like a heated coin. I was greeted by chamberlains on jewelled horses carrying gold brocade, silks, and carpets for the return voyage. They have dressed me in white robes and embroidered slippers. How I long for Finsbrekken, my mother's arms, the taste of cloudberries and codfish! The man to whom I am betrothed is tall and moustached, turbaned and scented. Of me he saw only my eyes, filled with tears. He bowed and thanked me for my father's gift. The wedding is appointed for the next high holy day, after the feast of Id al-Fitr.

Painting crosses on the Easter buns, Gabriela noticed they took on elaborate curlicued shapes, like something out of an old church. Fragments of a melody she didn't remember hearing ran through her head, the words in an unknown language: *Sofna, barn, sofna, Haldit í furu vaggunni þinni.* A customer, hearing her humming one morning, told her the tune was a lullaby she hadn't heard since her own mother sang it at her cradle in Oslo. At night after baking, Paul asleep beside her, she slapped her cheeks to stay awake, forced her eyelids apart, stood at the open window with the cool air on her face. If she slept she would walk again along tiled corridors, under curved archways, through the garden of walnut and quince and pomegranate to the high brick walls that shut out the desert.

When she fell asleep early one morning in the shop and scalded her hand in a pan of boiling water, the doctor diagnosed exhaustion and ordered her to bed. Paul brought her sleeping pills, hot milk, rum and lemon. Her eyes grew wide with fever, her cheeks burned. On the third day she fell asleep in the middle of a sentence and tumbled down into a warm cave where she curled like a hibernating bear. She slept for a day and a night and woke ready to run a marathon, her hand healed. Minna held out her arms to be picked up and Paul whistled as he grabbed his paintbrush and ran upstairs.

That night, the loaves in the oven, Minna asleep in the roasting pan she now occupied, Gabriela sat down to write a letter to her sister. The words flowed backwards out of her pen in a curved and graceful script, sentence after sentence that stopped only when she lifted the pen from the paper. Trembling, she tore up the letter. Next day she retrieved it from the waste basket, taped it together, and took it to a professor in the department of modern languages. Most peculiar, he said. An early example of the language. Note the presence of case endings and the use of the word *mizhar*. Where did you get this? And he accused her of stealing from the rare manuscripts in the library. She ran out the door before she could ask what the words meant.

What was she becoming? She was Gaby, ordinary Gaby, her life grounded in Paul, the baby, the milky smell of flesh, bread rising in the ovens. When she read a book the words ran together in flowing curves, the pages turned backwards. She no longer trusted herself to write, to speak, to sing. At night she rode in a *chador* through the sand dunes, palm trees and a cluster of white houses in the distance. She woke dizzy from heat, her throat parched, sand leaking from her fist. Even Paul noticed her sweat-soaked sheets, her deepening tan. Told her she talked in a strange language in her sleep, and not to lean so close to the ovens.

At night I lie awake, the scent of rosewater drifting through the open latticework, and smell again the pines in the forest round Finsbrekken, watch the snow falling on the frozen lake. I rode for miles wrapped in my cape, my horse steaming, bells jingling in the frosty air. On St. Olav's Day we went to mass in the small wooden church in the forest, knelt on the snowy doorstep and received blessing, mountain bluebirds alighting on the roof to peck at the crumbs tossed there by the priests.

Perhaps she was simply going crazy. Perhaps the walls contained a hitherto unknown chemical which leaked into her brain as she slept. A friend suggested a diet of eggs and lemons. Eggs and lemons contained tryptothamomine which induced vivid dreams, said an article in the newspaper. Another friend said the source of her dreams was the muscle and sinew of animals, she should give up meat. Eat raw liver, it's strengthening, whispered an elderly Czech lady in the shop. She spent a weekend in bed while Paul brought her bowls of soup and played with Minna, but the soup rocked in the bowl like a stormy sea and the bread tasted of sand. At night she pummelled the dough fiercely, doubled the recipe, found herself making *fatira* and *baklava* with narcissus and almonds. Paul had moved on from coyotes to landscapes, misty and moonlit, and customers spoke of restlessness, itchiness, a longing to travel. So they grew hungrier, and currant loaves, cheese bread, pepper rolls and challah flowed out of the kitchen into their mouths. Gabriela staggered back and forth with trays under her arms, piled on her head, knee-deep on the floor. Slept curled by the ovens in a country where servants brought her platters of roast lamb, scented wine, figs and olives.

She woke one morning to Minna crying. Buried there among the pans of doughnuts, the loaves of apple bread, she hadn't noticed how Minna was growing, how her round belly was bursting the snaps on her pyjamas and a chip of white tooth had worked its way through the pink gums. Gabriela walked up and down the kitchen rocking her, but Minna just cried harder. She even tried singing the strange lullaby, but the baby thrashed her fists and opened her mouth so wide Gabriela was afraid she'd disappear. She and Paul took turns rocking and holding, holding and rocking. The doctor gave them bottles of pink pills, jars of blue lotion. By evening the sobbing was quieter, punctuated by hiccups. Gabriela sat pushing the cradle with her foot, watching the baby's flushed cheeks, damp forehead. Please, sweetie, sleep. Sleep, baby, sleep. *Sofna, barn, sofna.*

My husband sits at my bedside and gives me nougat with his own hands, but I am not hungry. I turn my face away and remember how my father took me ice-fishing on a distant lake. How we sat for hours crouched over the hole, the line in my frozen mitts, and how a family of wolves came down to the tree-line to watch. And how good the fish tasted when we

*roasted it over an open fire, the sparks flying up among the
snowflakes.*

I am not hungry. I turn my face away.

In the middle of the night Minna turned blue and stopped
breathing. Paul shook Gabriela awake, wrapped Minna in a
blanket and forced air into her mouth while Gabriela called the
ambulance. At the hospital they placed Minna in a glass tank
sprouting tubes and wires. The air shimmered with fluorescent
light, the corridors smelled of bleach and floor polish. All night
Minna hovered in the tank, eyes closed, deciding between an
earthly and a heavenly existence. Gabriela wept, remembering
the overproduction of pepper rolls, her feverish kneading. Oh,
to be able to knead air and life into that tiny body! Paul paced up
and down the corridor, staring at his shoes, orderlies and nurses
veering round him like white corpuscles.

Three days later they took Minna home. She was pale and
her cheeks were creased with exhaustion, but the fever had
passed. They laid her in the big bed, blankets tucked round her
so she wouldn't roll off. Gabriela fed her milk with an eyedrop-
per, slid pills rolled in butter under her tongue. Paul tiptoed in
and out with fresh sheets, diapers, cups of tea. Hung a sign saying Closed Until Further Notice on the shop door and draped a
sheet over the painting on his easel.

*My husband consulted physicians, alchemists, soothsay-
ers, priests. Spent hours among dusty volumes and illuminated manuscripts in his library. My blood was too thick for
this country, they said, and so they administered leeches,
poultices, herbs. Gave me crushed rosepetals in a goblet of
water from an ice-fed spring in the mountains. I spat out the
petals and lapped at the water like a cat, bathed my face and
hands, asked for more.*

Days passed. Minna lay as though carved in ivory, her chest
rising and falling, eyes closed. Gabriela visited a herbalist, a
naturopath, a witch. Brought home rosemary and aloe and willow twigs, boiled them in the dusty kitchen and placed the
steaming pot by Minna's bed. Minna coughed and spluttered,

even opened her eyes for a moment while her colour rose. Then it faded again and she lay as before, a wax doll.

If only she hadn't been distracted by the curly crosses, the backward handwriting, the foreign lullaby! Gabriela slept in her clothes now, woke hungry and thin, her ribs aching. Ate furtively in the kitchen – stale *babka*, leftover crusts – while the shop bell rang insistently and voices called outside the door. While Paul sat upstairs cutting rocking horses out of paper, hung them at the foot of the bed.

My husband ordered wagons of snow from abroad. In the courtyard they melted, water dripping over the turquoise tiles. At midnight, when the temperature dropped below freezing, he woke me to look at the new skating rink. But by morning it had turned to water again. I pressed my face to the wall and tasted icicles, felt snowflakes thickening my lashes.

I am so thin I can count my ribs, one by one.

One day the ring of the doorbell was followed by hammering and pounding. It might be dangerous for Minna to be jarred out of her long sleep. Gabriela spat out a piece of mouldy bread and ran to the door. Why, it was the professor of modern languages, standing there with her piece of paper in his hand! After much searching he had tracked her down – never mind how, though it seemed to have something to do with the odour that had lingered in his office – and he wished to offer his most profound apologies. The piece of paper, on translation, had proved to be the missing fragment of a famous fourteenth-century manuscript known to have been composed by the poet Al-Rusafi, who had been commissioned by a certain Jabir ibn Khaldun, a nobleman noted for his interest in horticulture and his library of fifty thousand volumes, to write a love poem in a thousand quatrains to his wife. The manuscript had been authenticated by a committee of scholars, and he had been delegated to ascertain the provenance of such a valuable find. How had it come into her possession? And did she know that the poem was a masterpiece with many references to the twelfth-century epic of Shirin, the story of the passion of a Zoroastrian king for his Christian wife, written by – ? But

Gabriela had seized the paper from his hand and for a second time torn it into pieces. She pointed a trembling finger at the door. My life has been ruined by this piece of paper, she said. Out! Get out! And when the professor didn't move fast enough she grabbed the nearest saucepan and threw it. Ducking, the professor flew out the door but stopped at a safe distance. I beg you to give me the fragments. It's of great importance to our understanding of – But Gabriela hurled mixing bowls, knives, loaf pans, anything within reach, and the professor ran to his car holding his briefcase like a shield.

Gabriela sat among the twisted pans and broken dishes with tears leaking between her fingers. Once there had been sunlight, jostle, the perfume of bread, a baby's shrieks. Now it had all turned to ashes and sawdust. She threw the fragments of paper into an oven and watched them burn and blacken. Swept up the broken crockery, posted a FOR SALE sign in the window, and locked the door of the shop for the last time.

For days now the gardens have been full of voices, oxcarts, the clink of spades. At night my husband comes into my room in the clothes of a peasant, dirt under his fingernails. He is replacing some of the walnut trees, he says, to try out a new theory of cross-pollination. He asks the nurse if I have eaten anything. I feign sleep.

They made a nest for Minna in the back of the car and drove away without a backward glance at the wheat-sheaves on the door or the cherry tree in the back yard. The road they took twisted up through mountains and over peaks like a curling ribbon. Unrolled finally in a village whose inhabitants said good morning in a strange dialect and drove the cows home every evening at five. Outside the village they found a tiny cabin where there was just room for a bed, a cot, and a table. The air was crisp, the clouds like cotton. After tucking Minna under her quilt Gabriela stood outside and watched the evening mountains burst into flame.

They rose at dawn and went to bed at sunset. Ate food from their childhoods: bread dipped in milk, egg custard, toast soldiers. Took turns walking along the winding goat paths and sitting with Minna. The baby's cheeks blossomed, once or twice she even seemed to smile. Gabriela slept through the night now, woke clear-eyed, the sheets no longer damp and twisted in her hands. The tiled courtyards, the splashing fountains, the muezzin's cry faded like a life she had once known but had left behind. When she dreamt it was of shelf after shelf of golden loaves, gleaming in sunlight. Her hands kneaded the air as she slept, sometimes waking Paul, who pulled the covers over her and went back to sleep.

When they woke one morning to snow knee-deep around the cabin and wind gusting through the chinks, Gabriela tucked extra quilts around Minna and Paul dug a path to the road. The next morning the snow had blotted out the windows and the path had vanished. They rationed themselves to a bowl of soup and half a potato a day. Piled logs on the fire, sang songs and told stories, the light flickering on Minna's face. Once Gabriela would have seen minarets and archways among the yellow flames, but now she saw only sparks and embers.

On the fifteenth day Paul dressed in three layers of clothing, forced open the door, and waded through the waist-deep snow in the direction of the village. Gabriela fed Minna the last of the soup, sang songs, chewed her fingernails. In the evening she placed a lamp in the window. At night the wind moaned like an animal and the firelight threw black fingers on the ceiling. Once she thought she heard Paul calling her name and ran to the door. In the morning the fire had gone out and her fingers were so cold she could barely strike a match.

My husband no longer visits me. He says he is too tired after working all day in the gardens. The nurse says he has lost interest because I am so pale and thin. I order her to stand at the window and tell me what he does. My husband has forbidden it, but – just once – she veils her eyes and hides behind the curtain. Whispers that she has never seen walnut trees like these, so strange and white. And that my husband must be a sorcerer.

The next day a blizzard opened its throat and blew snow down the chimney. The water in the bucket froze solid.

Gabriela sat with Minna pressed against her, reciting nursery rhymes, lullabies, prayers. *Sofna, barn, sofna.* Minna's face was as pale as the light that filtered through their windows. They would turn into shadows, their bones fought over by wild animals when spring came. *Sofna, barn, sofna. Haldit í furu vaggunni þinni.*

From somewhere she could smell pine needles, damp wool, roasting fish. She could hear the jingling of bells on a bridle, the baying of dogs, strange voices calling. The room grew darker, the fire crackled and flared. She bent her head lower over Minna. What was this wet stain on her blouse? Her breasts were tingling, itching, swelling as they had done when she was pregnant. She undid the buttons with shaking fingers, lifted Minna to a nipple and watched as her eyes flew open and the small mouth seized and tugged. And when the baby had fallen back into flushed sleep, a dribble of milk at the corner of her mouth, Gabriela squeezed what was left into a glass and drank.

Tonight the movement and voices outside my window have stopped. My husband comes into my room, smiling. You cannot return to your land, he says, so I have brought snow to ours. He lifts me in his arms and carries me to the window.

In the middle of the night Gabriela wakes. She is so weak from hunger she can hardly stand, but she walks to the window and looks out. As far as she can see in every direction are cherry trees, thousands of them, their white blossoms floating against the night sky, the ground beneath them a thick carpet. She picks up Minna, who stirs but does not wake, opens the door and steps outside. Petals cover her arms, her hair, fall on Minna's upturned face. There is someone in the distance, calling, waving – is it Paul? As she strains to see through the falling blossoms Minna opens her eyes and smiles. If only he arrives in time to see this! She waves back, dizzy with the scent, the baby reaching out a fat fist to the white petals.

COUNTING

ON EASTER SUNDAY, dressed for church, my mother wears her new navy hat at an angle, its netting pulled over her forehead. I wear a straw sailor with a red ribbon and elastic under the chin. My sister Pamela, two years younger, has one with a blue ribbon. My baby brother, aged two, wears an aviator helmet in brown corduroy.

My mother also wears the dress I like best, a navy and white linen sheath with Chinese figures. She puts on powder and rouge and a French perfume with lilies of the valley on the label. Daddy bought it for her after an argument. Her silk stockings make a hushing sound as she wheels Billy down the street in his push-chair.

Today my father is coming with us too. He wears a dark suit and a tartan tie and combs his hair with Brylcreem. He locks the front door and then we all walk up the avenue together. My father walks very fast and tells me and Pamela to hurry up. When we get near the church in Stand Lane he takes over the push-chair from my mother. He grins and nods at people as we pass. 'Hello, Stan. Stopping by the pub after?' I look at my mother's face, watching for the tiny frown that appears between her eyebrows.

Usually he is away selling vacuum cleaners. Sunday is his best day, he says, he can go to the pub at dinnertime and meet half a dozen new customers. At teatime my mother says, 'You're setting a fine example for the children, in the pub on Sundays.'

'You don't complain about the pay packet, do you?' says my father. He pushes his chair back roughly, leaves the table. My mother looks at me, her mouth tight.

I am suddenly awake, listening, holding my breath. My father's angry voice, then a door slams right underneath me. Then my mother's voice, much fainter. He will wake Billy, then shout at Billy for crying. Think of anything, anything, arithmetic quiz, buttered scones, my new shoes, bruise on my knee where I fell off my bicycle, my teacher says good work Jill this essay shows – Slam. I force myself to lie on my stomach, ready for sleep, my face pressed into the pillow, but my head is lifted slightly to catch the words I don't want to hear. I hear Pamela move in the next bed and I know she is awake, but we don't say anything.

It is April, I have just turned nine. In the evenings I stand on the front gate beside the laburnum tree, looking up and down the avenue and eating licorice. One evening my mother calls me in early. I follow her into the gloom of the dining room where my father sits, smiling. My mother's face is puffy and she is turning her wedding ring round and round on her finger.

'We're moving to Canada,' says my father. I don't say anything. I tug at one of the heavy crocheted loops of the table-cloth. My mother's hand descends to pull mine away.

'Can I take Peter?' I ask. Peter is my blue-and-yellow budgie. At that moment I can't think of anything else I will miss. 'Probably Auntie Edna will –' says my mother, but my father says, 'Marjorie.' Like that, warningly, looking at my mother. To me he says, 'Maybe. We'll have to see.'

I am told not to tell Pamela yet, she is too little and won't understand. Also that Daddy will leave soon and find a job there before sending for us. 'Can I tell Vivienne?' I ask. Vivienne is my best friend. Her mother is an actress and wears red nail polish and big hats with feather plumes. 'Wait a while,' says my mother. 'Why not, it's all decided,' says my father. He just had his hair cut and looks very handsome, his eyes crease as he smiles at me. My mother says 'Ted' in a choked voice and goes out of the room. I go back outside and stand on the gate, swinging it slowly back and forth as my arms go pimply in the cold.

We live in a red brick semi-detached, joined to the next house by a sort of tunnel we call the passage. In rainy weather my sister and I play there. When it's fine we hang over the back fence to talk to Christopher and Rosalind in the next garden. Christopher is eight, thin and sickly, often indoors.

Rosalind is six. She has blonde hair in ringlets, her mother ties it up with rag strips at night. They have a playhouse under the beech tree in their garden, cupboards filled with tiny cups and saucers. We don't play there often, though, my mother thinks their mother is common. Also that she seems to have a lot of men friends. Their mother has a heart-shaped face and pencilled eyebrows, and wears very high heels when she goes out, which is almost every night.

We live on a street called Litchfield Avenue, which is full of other red brick houses just like ours. At one end is the waste ground, and far away at the other end, beyond the railway bridge, is the high street. There are rats on the waste ground. Round the corner is the way to school, and up towards the high street is the way to Auntie Edna's. Litchfield Avenue is in Swinnerton, which my mother says was just a village when she was a little girl. It isn't even on the map at school. All those streets and houses, hundreds and hundreds of houses, and the school and the toffee factory and Auntie Edna's and the Methodist Church, and there's not even a tiny dot on the map. Manchester, which is half an hour away by bus, has a big red dot. But it is smaller than the red patch which is London, and London is only a small piece of England, and England is smaller than France or Germany, and all of Europe could be swallowed up by Canada.

When I lie awake in bed and think about all this, about the hundreds of houses squeezed into one red dot, I have to stop because I get scared.

Monday is wash-day and Tuesday is ironing. Wednesday is dusting and vacuuming, Thursday is shopping, Friday is special jobs like cleaning the silver. Saturday mornings my mother bricks the front steps. She kneels on the second step with a bucket of hot water and wipes the steps with a wet cloth. Then she takes the cream-coloured donkeystone and rubs it like a cake of soap over the wet concrete. Sometimes she lets me do it, a chalky powder left on my fingers. At the end she wrings out the cloth and smooths the bricking so that it's even with no lines. On Saturdays the steps at each front door are freshly done in white or cream. Some are edged only, a white stripe running round the rim of each grey step.

At school I am silent. At night I dream I am a lake with a stone dropped in the middle, ripples widening outwards. I long to say we are moving to that snow-covered land in our text-books where Raoul the lumberjack and Jacques the coureur de bois live. I will fly on a plane, meet live Indians. Giving up my aunts and the playhouse does not seem too large a sacrifice. We go up to Liverpool on the train to see an immigration officer. A job interview for Daddy, my mother tells Pamela. I look at a large poster which shows rolling wheat-fields with a tiny red tractor in the middle and underneath in big white letters: Canada – Land of Opportunity.

My father is to take me and Pamela into Manchester on Saturday afternoon to see the ice skaters at the Palladium. Pamela wears her best pink cotton frock and I wear my grown-up dress, green with a white collar and bow. My father gives me his arm as we walk down the street. There is a queue outside the Palladium and Pamela hops from one foot to the other. Inside the lobby it is dim and crowded. Pamela squeezes my hand. Daddy tells us to wait and pushes through to the brightly lit counter where they sell ice cream and sweets. He comes back with a bag of Pontefract cakes and a packet of imitation cigarettes. The cigarettes are for Billy, he says, the Pontefract cakes are for me and Pamela to share.

We go up the thick carpeted stairs to the balcony and get seats right at the front. Below us brightly coloured skaters glide and twirl on the ice. When I lean over the air is cold on my face. I watch a tall man and lady, holding hands with their arms crossed in front, skating slowly and gracefully round the outside edge. A lady in pink with a pink feathered hat is spinning in the middle, slowly at first, then faster and faster so her skirt stands straight out and you can see frilly lace panties underneath. Pamela giggles and I frown at her. 'Stare, stare, like a bear, she's got dirty underwear,' says Pamela in my ear. 'What are you girls whispering about?' says my father.

It's a long long way down to the skating rink. I bite off a piece of Pontefract cake, lean over, and let it drop, just like that. Finally it hits the ice, a tiny black speck. Then I think, suppose someone gets their skate stuck on it? The pink lady or the gliding couple? And I can't watch any more. Any minute now I'll hear a crash on the ice and I cover my ears. 'Are you cold?' says my father. 'Here,' he says, and he rubs my ears with his hands.

'In Canada there's lots of ice-skating,' he says. 'You girls will probably learn.'

'Oh no,' says Pamela. 'I'd fall down.'

I see Pamela and me wearing fur muffs and skating over a frozen lake, wearing long dresses like the pictures of skaters on Christmas cards. Perhaps we will live on a lake and skate to school and back. The lake grows larger. There is just lake and snow and forest and sky, and me and Pamela in the middle, skating on as the snow begins, our hands toasty warm in our muffs.

My father leaves soon after. We stand in the hallway early one morning, Pamela and me in our plaid dressing gowns, my mother in her pink satin one. A clear cool morning in June, the front door is open and I can see pale blue sky over my father's shoulder. He is standing between two brown leather suitcases, wearing his tweed overcoat (it might be cold there, he says) and a brown peaked motoring cap. My mother is holding Billy and trying not to cry. 'I'll probably run off and join an Indian tribe,' he says, and laughs. A car horn sounds at the gate. Still smiling he kisses us all quickly. His moustache scratches across my cheek. He hurries down the path. The taxi door opens and shuts. Billy bounces up and down in my mother's arms and waves his hands. The taxi is gone. This goodbye does not feel any different from the others. My mother blows her nose and picks up the milkbottle from the step, its foil top left ragged by birds.

My father writes long letters, squeezed black writing I can't read on crinkly blue paper. The stamps have the Queen's face on them, like ours, blue instead of orange. In the evening after Pamela has gone to bed I drink cocoa with my mother and she reads them aloud.

'Dearest Marjorie, How are my girls? Landed in Vancouver at 5:05 yesterday afternoon in pouring rain after a long tiring flight, nearly 13 hours with the refuelling stop in Gander. The customs officer said we were the third planeload of British immigrants that day. Sat next to a chap called Eric Bishop who used to sell machine tools for Davis Bros. in Manchester. We're rooming together at a hotel called the Admiral which has porthole-shaped windows. Eric jokes about getting seasick if we have a beer. We're in good company down at the labour exchange, two fellows from Leicester and another group from Leeds. Not much in the way of selling jobs, though. Tomorrow I have an interview with a firm which sells medicines – drugs they're called here. Saw my first Indian today, unfortunately he was a bit under the weather –' (my mother stops and glances at me) '– but that is usually the way I'm told. Cheerio for now and best love to all, Ted.'

One day my mother opens the door to a short man in a rain-coat, sandy hair, scuffed brown shoes. 'My name's Eric Bishop,' he says. My mother catches her breath and glances at the front gate. 'I came back by myself,' he says, straightening his tie. 'There's no jobs in Vancouver. But Ted decided to have a go further north, we heard there were logging jobs with a couple of the big forest companies. Pays well but the work's a bit too dicey for me I'm afraid. He left by train a week ago. Asked me to look you up.'

'Logging!' says my mother. Dangerous, dirty, your father deserves better, she says. 'You're not to tell Auntie Edna,' she says, and then does so herself the next day when my aunt drops by unexpectedly. The same day I tell Vivienne that my father is on a secret mission. 'In Hungary,' I say, news of the Hungarian Revolution is in the papers. Vivienne lends me the amethyst ring her grandmother gave her, which I lose down the bath drain the next day and so end our friendship. Also a *Daily Mirror* which tells how Eartha Kitt was tied up as a child by her stepfather and whipped across the bare buttocks. My mother won't allow the *Daily Mirror* in the house.

'20th July. Dearest Marjorie, As I write this I'm sitting in the rec room of the men's bunkhouse for Crown Zellerbach in Terrace. Talked my way into a job as a chokerman on Friday after a fourteen-hour train journey from Prince George. Train before ours was derailed when it hit a moose! Yesterday morning saw my first black bear outside the cookhouse. It ambled away into the bush but that night we heard scuffling noises outside the back door. The Pole who sleeps in the bunk above me yelled at it through the window, but evidently it didn't understand Polish so I poked at it with a broom handle and after a growl or two it left! Today was a real scorcher – ninety odd and I could have wrung out my wool shirt when we got back to camp. Word is they may be closing the forests down soon due to fire danger. If so think I will head northwest to the new aluminum smelter on the coast at a place called –'

'I can't read the name,' says my mother. 'Anyway that's the end of the letter.'

'But there's another page,' I say.

'Just about grown-up things. Do you know what time it is? Run along to bed right this minute.'

August. A heat wave. Pamela and I look almost alike in our cotton dresses, white sandals, bare brown legs, except that she is shorter, chubbier, blonder. On Sundays at dinnertime when the ice cream bell sounds I am sent out with a chipped enamel jug to have it filled with vanilla ice cream. I am just tall enough to grip the countertop of the open window with my fingers. I can feel the cool metal sides of the van through my skirt. The ice cream man pours raspberry vinegar over the jugful of ice cream. He has thick greasy hair and a gold tooth. He hands me back the jug and my change, then grabs my hand and stares at me before letting go. I run inside, my face hot, my back prickling. 'It's the heat,' I tell my mother when she looks at me.

There hasn't been a letter for a long while. My mother says not to worry, Daddy is probably working hard, and looks worried. The next time she writes I write too, about Christopher and Rosalind's new kitten and how Billy can now open the china cabinet.

It is very quiet. At night there are no angry voices. In the evenings I read *Jane of Lantern Hill* to my mother while she knits. Jane lives in Prince Edward Island and worries about getting her grades. I ask my mother what that means but she doesn't know. When the doorbell rings we both jump and look at each other.

One day we go down the street to the Simmonses to use their phone. I stand beside my mother in the kitchen lacing and unlacing my fingers while she says my father's name into the phone and then shouts it. There is a lot of static, she says, she can't hear very well. She says 'Yes, Ted Carruthers,' and then 'How long ago?' and then 'Yes, I'm his wife.' When she hangs up Mrs. Simmons offers us tea and says, 'How is he?'

'I just missed him,' says my mother. 'He's on his way to another camp. It's very kind of you but I left Billy with Pamela.' She walks home very fast holding my hand, I have to run to keep up. In the house she says, 'He left three weeks ago and there's no forwarding address. I won't ever forgive your father for this, Jill.' She bangs the cupboard door. Billy begins to cry.

When I was little my mother painted my bedroom ceiling blue and stuck silver paper stars all over. At night, Pamela asleep, I open the curtains a little and the stars catch the light from the streetlamp outside. I count the stars slowly. When I finish the doorbell will ring and my father will be there, laughing, holding presents. Or in the morning there will be a letter saying, Come right away. I arrange the stars into rows, diagonals, count up and down. Perhaps if I count them in twos or threes, count every third star and then start over. I must do this for my mother, and Billy, and Pamela. So I count, and in the morning the stars are a dull silver again, and my mother says we'll catch our death of cold leaving the window open all night like that.

On Saturdays we visit Auntie Edna. My mother puts Billy in his push-chair and we walk up the avenue and under the railway bridge to the high street. Past Bentley & Son Greengrocers, past Boots' Chemists and the sweetshop, rows of jars with silver lids, to Old Lyme Road where we turn right. Past

Hall's Toffee Works with its warm sweet smell, cauldrons pouring a thick gleaming brown stream into moulds. Under the chestnut trees at the edge of the park with the black metal hobbyhorses and the Peter Pan statue. After the last houses there are fields with daisies in them. We go through a stile and follow a cowpath which comes out in Wheaton Crescent, where my aunt lives.

Today my aunt is standing in the kitchen with flour streaks in her hair making buns and custard for dinner. My mother takes a pile of newspapers off a chair and sits down to talk. She holds Billy on her lap but he struggles down and my aunt gives him a saucepan and wooden spoon to play with. I go in the living room and lie on my stomach and read my *Girls' Adventure Annual*. Anne and Diana, fourth-formers at St. Swithin's, are about to unmask the hooded figure who nightly roams the school corridors.

The clock in the dining room seems very loud. I get up and go through the dining room, and stop. My mother is sitting with her face against my aunt's apron and my aunt is bending over her, stroking her hair. My mother's shoulders are shaking. My aunt looks up and sees me. 'Just your mother's nerves, lovey. Now run along, dinner'll be ready in a jiffy.'

October. Everything is brown – the leaves, my pleated uniform, smoke from the smokestacks at the mill down by the waste ground. We play skipping in the schoolyard at break. Pamela joins the line of girls but I hold one end and am a never-ender. As the rope curves overhead Pamela runs in, then jumps and it sails under her feet.

> *Down in the meadow where the green grass grows*
> *There sat Pamela as pretty as a rose.*
> *She sang, she sang, she sang herself to sleep,*
> *And up came Colin and kissed her on the cheek.*

'When you go to Canada,' says Geoffrey, coming up to me, 'will you live in a cabin or a hut?' Geoffrey is one of the class monitors. 'We're not going to Canada,' I say. My face is hot. Pamela has finished her turn and is standing looking at us.

'Your father's in Canada,' says Geoffrey. 'My dad says your dad's a bounder.'

'Fibber. You're a fibber,' says Pamela.

'My dad says your dad ran off to the colonies because he couldn't make a go of it here.'

'Your ears stick out,' says Pamela. 'Did you know that? They stick out like this,' and she puts her hands behind her ears and waggles them forwards and backwards.

'Your dad's just jealous,' I say, 'because he isn't chopping down trees and fighting bears like my dad.'

'Yeah, and my dad's the King of England,' Geoffrey says, and walks away.

'Snotnose,' says Pamela under her breath. 'Snotnose.'

November. Everything has changed. My mother has a job. She leaves the house at seven, while it is still dark. I wake to her bending over me, scent of her Yardley's talcum powder, her rabbit fur collar brushing my face. Then the front door opens and shuts. I get up and wake Pamela, go into Billy's room where he sits on the bed in his pyjamas running his Dinky cars over the counterpane. He can almost dress himself except for buttoning the straps of his overalls. Going downstairs he holds the banister and pulls his other hand out of mine. My mother sets the table before she goes, yellow plates and Billy's mug, the tea still warm. I make toast and Pamela tips cornflakes into bowls. Holding the elastics in my mouth I braid her hair, button the back of her dress. Sometimes she won't do what I tell her. 'Clear the table, Pamela,' I say as I put Billy's jacket on. 'You're not my mother,' she says. Once she gave me a push and knocked Billy against the chair, his lip started bleeding. 'Now look what you've done,' I said. 'Just wait till I tell Mummy.' Pamela backed away then, ran upstairs crying.

We take Billy to Mrs. Markham's round the corner, then walk to school, our satchels over our raincoats.

We stay for lunch now. We stand in lines in the big dining hall and hold thick grey-white plates. Monday is toad-in-the-hole, Tuesdays is mince, Wednesdays is beans on toast. I don't like any of them. Under the gravy there are tiny little cracks like rivers in the plate. I am certain thousands of invisible insects live in the cracks. The girl next to me talks thickly through her food with her mouth open. Sometimes the mistress at the head of the table bangs her plate with a spoon and tells us to keep the noise down.

Some days Pamela and I walk home together. Other days I walk home with Lynne Matthews who lives up the street and Pamela walks with the Reilly twins who are her best friends. When we get home at four my mother is always there, slicing bread and humming, the kettle on to boil. Bits of thread cling to the blue smock she has thrown over a chair. 'I've had to rehem that Emperor's costume three times,' she says, or 'Millie and I had another row with the wardrobe mistress, I keep telling her it's not right the girls have to supply their own thimbles and pincushions.' Sometimes she sings songs from the latest production. 'Three little maids from school are we,' she sings, or 'The flowers that bloom in the spring.' She says she can't do them justice, that she'll get tickets for me and Pamela and Auntie Edna and Uncle John to go one night. When I open the door my mother is always there, and I stop being afraid.

One day when I get home from school there is no one in the kitchen, voices in the living room. I push open the door from the hallway. There is a man sitting on the couch next to my mother. He has sad eyes pulled downwards by thick slanted eyebrows, a little black moustache, wavy black hair. He wears a suit and tie, holds our best china cup and saucer. He puts down the cup as I enter and stands up. My mother sits forward on the edge of the couch, smiling, holding the rose-patterned teapot in midair. She still wears her blue working smock. Her cheeks are red. She says, 'Jill, this is Mr. Karolaitis.'

'Nick,' says the man, and holds out his hand to me. I think this is silly, me shaking hands with him. His hand is large, fat, warm, with black hairs on the back and a thick gold ring on the fourth finger. 'My eldest daughter, Jill, the one who's such a help,' says my mother, looking up at him. She asks me if I would like tea. Mr. Karolaitis is a carpenter at the theatre, she says. He is looking at me and shaking his head. 'I thought you were all little,' he says, in a strange accented voice deeper than my father's. 'I have brought gifts but they are for very little ones.' He takes a wrapped package out of a large paper bag beside the couch. I can feel my mother watching me as I open it, so I say 'Oh, how lovely!' as soon as I take the paper off. It is a toy duck with a wind-up key. 'I am sorry, you are a young lady already, I did not know,' he says.

'Nick, you shouldn't have,' says my mother. She frowns a little at me. I say thank you and stand there holding the present. My mother says, 'Could you go and see where Billy is, he was here a moment ago.'

I leave the room. Billy is sitting on the kitchen floor, his hands and face covered with jam from the open jam pot beside him. I wind up the yellow duck and take the jam pot away. The duck quacks and waddles forward. Billy laughs and picks it up, his fingers sticky on the duck's yellow fur.

It is almost Christmas. A green Christmas this year, says my mother. Pamela thinks she means no turkey for Christmas dinner, only vegetables. My mother says Mr. Karolaitis has tickets for the pantomime, would we like to go. 'Are you coming too?' I ask. 'Yes, of course,' says my mother. 'Aren't you pleased?'

'He talks in a funny way,' I say.

'That's because he's Greek,' says my mother. 'He speaks very good English for someone who's only been here a few years.'

'Isn't he married?' I ask.

My mother pauses. 'He had to leave his wife and little girl behind when he escaped after the war. And he lost touch with them. He says his little girl would be about your age now. Her name's Anastasia.'

On the day of the pantomime I say I don't feel well. There are funny red spots on my tongue when I look at it in the mirror. Probably tomorrow I will really be sick. My mother feels my forehead. 'You don't have a fever but perhaps you'd better stay in bed just in case. Will you be all right on your own?'

She comes in again after lunch to say goodbye and tuck me in. She has on her pearl earrings and fresh make-up. 'I won't kiss you, I'll smudge my lipstick. See you later, love.' Pamela lends me her big doll with real hair.

I breathe on the frosty window and watch them get into a small blue car and drive away. I trace the curls and waves of frost with my fingers. Here is England and that big patch is Canada and over there is Greece. I stick my finger on Greece and try to imagine a country where it is always hot and sunny. Olive groves and white houses and in one of them is Anastasia. She has dark curly hair and a sad smile. I will write a letter and we will be pen-pals. Perhaps I'll invite her to visit and when she comes, what a surprise.

When they come home I pretend I am asleep, but I hear them downstairs, my mother making tea and laughing. After awhile I hear Pamela and Billy playing in Billy's bedroom next door. Downstairs there are voices and silence, voices and silence. My mother isn't laughing any more. I hear music on the gramophone, when I open the door it is the Arthur Phipps Orchestra playing 'When You Go Home Tonight, Adeline.' My mother taught me how to waltz to this tune. Does Anastasia waltz with her mother too? Soon the music will end and he will go. I will hold my breath and when I stop, he will go.

The music stops. My mother is laughing. I go back in the bedroom and shut the door.

February. A whooping cough epidemic at school. I get it and then Pamela. My mother worries about Billy. She makes little balls of soft butter and rolls them in sugar. Grandma's remedy, she says. Leaves a plate of them in our room at night.

I want to take ballet lessons but she says she can't afford them.

She asks if I will mind being on my own for an evening with Billy and Pamela, she is going to the pictures with some friends from work. 'You won't be afraid, will you?' she says. 'I won't be late.'

She goes out smelling of perfume and I see the little blue car drive away.

After Pamela goes to bed I make tea and feel grown up. I walk from the kitchen to the hallway to the living room. The doorbell will ring and it will be my father, his arms full of presents.

'Would you like some tea?' I ask. He sits in front of the fire and warms his hands, and I bring him tea and fry bacon and eggs. 'Where's your mother?' he says.

'At the pictures. But she'll be home soon.'

'That's my girl,' he says as I give him his plate and refill his cup. And he tells me about forests and mountains and fording rivers on log rafts, and Mounties chasing criminals on snowshoes, and how he got the bearskin rug that he's brought home.

When my mother comes in she will say, 'What a good thing you were here to greet your father, Jill. Hello, Ted,' and he will kiss her and smack her bottom, just like he used to.

March. Pamela and I roller-skate up and down outside on the pavement. My mother says when will I stop growing, none of my summer frocks from last year fit me even if she lets the hems down. Pamela is sulking because she has to wear my old spring coat from two years ago.

I go to Lynne Matthews' birthday party, eight of us see *Sleeping Beauty* at the Odeon and then have dishes of ice cream at a posh restaurant. It is late when Mr. Matthews drops me off at the gate. In the dark hallway I almost stumble over two suitcases. The door to the living room opens and a tall man with a beard stands there, wearing a funny peaked cap with New York Yankees written on it. He bends down and picks me up, and he smells strange and familiar and it is my father. I am too big to be picked up and I wriggle down, tugging at my skirt. He laughs and calls me honey and I pull away and go to my mother. My mother puts her hand on my head and says, 'You can't really blame her, can you?'

'It'll be fine, you'll see,' says my father. 'Don't be mad, Jill. Look, I brought you a present, and some candy, that's Canadian for sweets. You'll be a big hit at school.'

'Not a single letter,' says my mother. 'Not a single letter for eight months, and then you turn up out of the blue, just like that.'

'Let's not quarrel the minute I arrive, Marjorie,' says my

father. 'I promise it'll all be explained later. Right now I want to say hello to my big girl.'

'You don't know what I've gone through, Ted,' says my mother, and begins to cry. She just stands there with the tears running down her chin and my father goes over to her and pulls her head to his shoulder.

'There, there, darling. I know you must have been very worried and I've been very naughty not to write. But just give me a chance to explain everything.'

My father pats her on the back until she stops crying. She dabs at her eyes with a hanky and my father takes her hand, then holds his other hand out to me. 'Come on, Jill, let's be friends. Your dad's home and everything'll be okay.'

I turn my head away. I turn my head away and go out of the room. 'Jill, honey,' calls my father. Liar liar pants on fire. My father is never coming back.

A door slams. I wake up. It is dark, no light in the room, and someone has covered me with a blanket. In the next bed I hear Pamela's slow breathing. I hear my father shout something, then my mother's voice, hurried, softer. Another slam, quick footsteps. The room is small and hot and the ceiling presses down on me. I get up and tiptoe over to Pamela's bed. She is asleep with the Indian doll my father brought.

Downstairs it is quiet. After a long time I open the bedroom door and stand on the landing, looking down. The lights are out, they have gone to bed. The two suitcases still stand in the hallway. Perhaps when I wake up in the morning they will be gone.

BOLT BOMB

SPLITTING WOOD in the yard, his breath a cloud around him, Boyd watched the ears of the old black Lab where she lay on the porch. As soon as Charlie was in whistling distance the ears would prick, head lift, and Boyd would hide the axe in the woodpile, sit at the kitchen table and open a magazine. Already the sky was purple, the pile of split logs knee-high beside him; Charlie should have been home hours ago. Boyd saw his brother sitting in the lawyer's office, face flushed under his trainman's cap, banging the desk with his good hand. The lawyer leafing through papers while Boyd lifted the axe high, sank it into the pine splitting cleanly in the cold air.

Leaning out the window of the bus last Wednesday on her way to her sister's, his mother had mouthed words at him: *Look after Charlie. Call me if the letter comes.* And he'd jerked his shoulders, watching Charlie load her suitcase into the baggage hold, had mouthed a promise back. But after the bus pulled away Charlie held up the stump with its leather sleeve, said Can't always be holding my hand, Boyd. Drove home laughing, the wheel in his fist, Boyd shifting gears, said now they could fill the fridge with beer, sleep late. When the letter came he'd sat rigid for an hour, gripping the paper, a muscle in his jaw flickering. Told Boyd it was his own business and he'd go to the lawyer's by himself. Still clumsy with his left hand he'd shaved, put on a clean shirt and even a tie, looking away while Boyd knotted it for him. At night sometimes he woke still, covered in sweat, shouting, Boyd's name or someone else on the crew. Once Boyd found him wandering the house at 2 a.m., weeping, half dragged half carried him back to bed. Charlie held his arms and wouldn't let go. We were kids, we were fishing, he whispered. Out on the lake by Sullivan's place. I was reeling in this huge trout, musta been twenty pounds, reeling her in with both hands. I almost fell in but you grabbed my legs and held me. He wept again, face turned away in the pillow, until Boyd said they'd go fishing in the old places next summer, buy a left-handed reel and they'd both learn.

The dog whined, lifting her head, ran from the yard with her tail beating. By the time Charlie opened the front door Boyd had the coffee on and fat spitting in the frying pan. He heard him talking to the dog, heard the thud of a body against the wall. Ran to find him pushing himself upright, clinging to the door-frame for support, his breath beery and sour on Boyd's face. Thought I wouldn't notice you out there, didn't you, he said, clutching Boyd's shirt. I told you a dozen times, I can do it as good as you. He stumbled across to the sofa and fell full length while Boyd knelt to unlace his boots. Lawyer made everything crystal clear, Boyd. Sitting there in his hundred-dollar shoes. Charlie pulled the crumpled envelope from his pocket and flung it at him. Sweet fuck all is what I'm getting. He lifted himself on an elbow, stabbed a finger in the air. Your fault, kiddo, is what the Board said. Your fault for fooling around on the job. So here I am, eighteen and all washed up. He fell back on the sofa, breathing heavily, and Boyd picked up the envelope. *Dear Mr. Fairfield, In reference to the above-mentioned claim, pursuant to an injury sustained in the course of your employment, and having reviewed all the evidence on file, the Board is of the unanimous opinion that ... hazard introduced into the workplace by the claimant and therefore the employer cannot be held responsible ... we regret to advise that claim is hereby denied yours truly.*

Boyd dropped the letter on the coffee table and stood up. Charlie's breathing had slowed, his good arm hung from the sofa. Outside it had begun to snow, great flakes that whirled under the streetlamp across the road.

People around town knew the battered red pickup, train whistle dangling from the rear-view, knew that one of the Fairfield boys would drive up in a spurt of gravel and swing down out of the cab. Railwaymen now for three generations, the Fairfields, from grandfather Isaac who'd lost an eye laying steel to his son Harry who'd died in the great Fort Lewis collision when a signalman, drunk on Christmas whisky, neglected to inform Harry at the controls that the 11:25

express out of Tillotsford was running twenty minutes late. Harry's death a Christmas present for his widow and two small boys, aged ten and eight. So it was no surprise when Boyd, the day after graduation, hired on at the local yard, though people said his mother had told him if he was brought home in a coffin one day she wasn't going to bury him. Boyd was a good worker, people said, steady, reliable. Charlie, the same year, quit school at sixteen, worked as a faller up the valley and a deck-hand down south, came home whistling after pitching overboard in a storm and being fished out nearly dead with a grappling hook. Which was only to be expected, since he'd tumbled out of a tree at four, swallowed rat poison at seven, at twelve playing with Tina McEvoy almost burned down her father's stable. Came home whistling and wrung out his clothes, played pool at the hotel, took a different girl every Saturday night to the pub in Millersville, worked around town some doing a little carpentry, construction, until July when the railway put up notices and Charlie went down to the yard one hot day and hired on. Same crew as Boyd, working on repairs up and down the line between Davis and Carlisle, a distance of a hundred miles, three seventy-two an hour and if he stayed long enough a brass plaque to put beside his father's on the mantelpiece.

As always they'd left the outfit car at 6 a.m. that day, carrying their lunch-boxes, steam already rising from the wet grass. They took the rail car fifteen miles down, waited for the 8:19 to Brantley to go through, then filled spike holes until noon, taking turns on the mallet, the smell of blistered tar in their nostrils. After lunch, stripped to the waist, they unloaded spare ties and track torpedoes off a work train caboose, stopping only to let the 2:57 go by, clean-shaven faces peering out over the white tabletops of the dining car.

Waiting for that last train they'd watched Jerry, how he'd screwed a nut part way onto a track bolt, filled the nut with powder from a torpedo, screwed a second bolt into the other side. Saw him lift his arm and throw, saw an explosion of sparks and metal against the caboose, a noise so loud Boyd felt it along his jaw, the dent left behind in the steel. Going back on the rail car Boyd watched Charlie's fist open on a couple of bolts, saw him pull a torpedo from the pile under the seat and tear the package with his teeth. Watched him pour the powder in a thin white stream into the nut, slide the second bolt into the thread and begin to turn. Don't tighten that thing, said Boyd, and Charlie's chin lifted the way it had at age five when Boyd found him lighting matches in their father's workshop. Don't, said Boyd, and turned his head away to check their distance from camp on a mileage post. Out of the corner of his eye he saw the flash, felt something sear his cheek as the sound went through him, whirled back as Charlie fell sideways into his lap, screaming, blood pouring from the severed vein in his neck and his right hand a jelly of flesh at Boyd's feet.

At the hospital, an eighty-mile trip over dirt roads, they worked four hours to pull jagged bits of metal from the stump, gave Charlie a transfusion of Boyd's blood because he'd lost so much. Boyd phoned a neighbour who walked down the road to tell their mother and was there to catch her when she fell, white-faced and silent, into his arms. Three days later they took a skin graft from Charlie's arm and laid a neat patch over the missing flesh in his neck. By then Charlie was sitting up, eating steak and joking with the nurses. The railway sent a vase bursting with roses. Charlie shared a ward with a logger, age twenty-seven, both legs lost below the knee. In physio they taunted each other, held bets, swore at the stiffened limbs and the imaginary feet and the fingers that still ached for motion. The logger gripped a leather belt between his teeth, lifted each wasted thigh as he sat on the bed, blood draining from his face. Charlie played piano scales with ghostly fingers, the therapist joining him on a duet.

When he came home Charlie sat for a week in the rocking chair by the window, refusing to eat. Then lined up tin cans on the backyard fence and every day for a month stood with the rifle against his left cheek, butt resting on his stump, aiming for those tin hearts. Went out after that and shot a rabbit, brought it home grinning, fed it to the dog.

Boyd woke next morning to grey blurred light and the sound of wood being chopped in the yard. Charlie stood there in his plaid shirt, sweating, the axe handle gripped in his left hand, the old Lab watching him, swinging her tail. He raised the axe above his head, brought it down and missed. Repositioned the log, raised the axe, missed again. Wiped his face as he jerked the axe out of the chopping block, lifted it, connected this time with the log which split neatly in two. He kicked the pieces aside into a separate pile from Boyd's, much smaller. Boyd let the curtain fall, turned away.

Charlie went out after breakfast with the dog and Boyd phoned the union office. Yes, they'd heard, a damn shame, though they'd warned Charlie that the Board was known to be tough on this type of case. They'd paid for Charlie's lawyer, done as much as they could. Meanwhile elections were coming up, would Boyd consider running as shop steward for the local? No, said Boyd, and hung up. A cousin in Vancouver knew a lawyer who specialized in compensation cases, but his office said he no longer did them on contingency and would need a four-thousand-dollar retainer, up front. Boyd stared out at the flurries eddying round the truck, remembering the massive oak table, the black suits, the fleshy faces. The questions, no one looking Charlie in the eye: *Could you explain again, Mr. Fairfield ...!* Charlie cradling the prosthesis in his lap, a spare one they'd had at the hospital when he went back for the operation to reshape the stump, thrown out later because it chafed him raw.

Charlie came back in the late afternoon, silent, sat in the fading light by the window with his fingers pressed to his eyes. Left the rocking chair bucking dangerously when Boyd tried to talk to him and went upstairs, slamming his door. Boyd found out later from someone on the crew that Charlie had turned up in Johnson's office, waving his letter, saying he'd been promised a desk job. A decent man, Johnson, remembered their father, *his* father had laid steel with their grandfather, but he didn't know anything about the Board's offer and besides, Charlie couldn't type, couldn't spell, wouldn't want to sit behind a desk in an office full of women, would he? So Charlie had shredded his letter onto Johnson's desk and walked out. Johnson had stood at the door and watched him go, had turned up at the Legion that evening and downed three straight whiskies one after the other, though everyone knew he wasn't a drinking man.

On Friday nights people came in from Millersville and Pemstock and Taylor, drawn by the dance floor at the hotel, the cheap beer, the faces of travellers passing through. Boyd arrived late with Charlie and found most of the crew at a table in the far corner, its surface already circled with wet. The beat from the band travelling along the floor and through Boyd's heels, drowning out whatever it was Jerry was shouting at him over the raised glasses.

They played eight-ball in the back room, leaning through the smoke above the green felt, all except Charlie who said no, he'd stay and have another beer. Boyd, waiting his turn, watched him slumped in his chair, staring out the black window into the parking lot. Once Charlie had pulled crowds to the circle of light, never failing to call the pockets, running the table so often no one inside fifty miles would play. Now he wouldn't touch a cue, said it was the one thing you needed two hands for.

When Boyd looked up again the table in the other room was empty. Charlie was on the dance floor, hand at the waist of a girl, red hair and a short dress. Talking rather than dancing, he leaning close to hear what she was saying. Sure hasn't stopped them coming round like moths, said Jerry, blowing smoke from the corner of his mouth. You gonna take your turn or what?

Her name was Lina and she'd come up for the evening with a couple of friends from Pemstock. She sat swinging a high-heeled shoe and curling a strand of hair round a finger. Her dad was a foreman at the Taylor mill, she said, Boyd thought he knew a brother on one of the rail crews. She studied business accounting at the college, worked nights as a waitress. Charlie sat with his boots on the table, sleeve touching hers, lower lip slack from a half-dozen beer. Boyd watched her touch the empty cuff of Charlie's jacket as Charlie raised his glass and said, To my big brother Boyd who looks after me so well. Set the glass down so fast it skidded against the bottle. I heard you made that trip to the hospital in under an hour, she said. If it had been my brother I would've passed out.

I never thought about it, Boyd said. She had small ears close to her head and a way of arching her neck when she laughed. When her girl-friends arrived, buttoning jackets, snapping purses, she squeezed Charlie's shoulder, her hair swinging down as she bent to kiss him on the cheek.

How you're gonna tickle her without fingers, Charlie? someone said after she'd left. Boyd put a hand out as Charlie swung his boots off the table, his eyes narrowed, said did any-one want another, he was paying for the next round. I still got five, Charlie said. Plus ten toes and a tongue. Just takes a little more imagination than you got.

At home, pitching up the stairs with Charlie's arm across his shoulder, Boyd said Keep this up and you'll have a gut like a pig before you're twenty. Charlie lay half on half off the bed while Boyd yanked at his jacket. You should have stuck around, Boyd. Stayed and had a beer with me instead of going off to play pool.

You'll think she'll stay in Pemstock? said Boyd. She's going to college, she's got plans. Just don't fall too hard, that's all.

Charlie turned down a job at the hardware store because, so he said, he didn't want old ladies patting his cheek while he dusted shelves. Mornings he built model airplanes, fitting the tiny pieces into place with his teeth, gripping the paintbrush in his left hand. Afternoons he slept. Coming off shift Boyd stood in the living room talking in a low voice to their mother, listening for any noise overhead. I'm a cripple, I can't do that, Charlie said when Boyd suggested they rebuild the truck motor together, insulate the attic. He was supposed to go to Vancouver to be fitted for a new prosthesis but kept delaying the appointment. Weekends he drove to visit Lina, came back with dark circles under his eyes. Took off his shirt in the upper hallway, his back turned so Boyd would notice the long scratches in the flesh.

In January the bartender at the hotel dropped a keg of beer on his foot and the manager, an ex-railwayman himself, asked Charlie if he'd like to fill in. Charlie polished highball glasses, shook ice and creme de menthe in metal shakers, learned to fill twenty mugs with draft in under thirty seconds. Practised balancing a tray of drinks on his stump when no one was looking, sat in his room memorizing ingredients from a book propped up on the barbells he no longer used. Sometimes Lina helped out on Friday nights, washed glasses or carried trays, her fingers interleaved with tens and twenties. At home he whistled sometimes, asked for seconds, watched hockey games on TV instead of leaving the room. Boyd found the model planes packed away in a box in the basement.

The doctor at the hospital sent Charlie a brochure on the latest type of prosthesis, a two-pronged claw which opened and closed by means of a battery. As good as new, the manufacturer said; the owner could pick up a pen and write, throw a ball, use a chain-saw. Charlie dropped the brochure on the dinner table one evening. He had money saved for the trip to Vancouver, would his mother go with him? He was sure his boss would give him the time off. Maybe, with the new hand, he could even hire on with the railway again.

Boyd was on a work train crew, delivering steel and ties between Tyrone and Boultby, coming into town weekends deaf from the roar of the crane. He and the crew sat at the usual table in the corner, ordered drinks from Lina who worked steady on weekends now. Late in the evening a fight blew up at the pool table, one of the local bikers and a thin-faced East Indian from the mill down the road. Drinks were spilled, a chair thrown. Rumours went round that the biker had a gun. Lina, coming off shift, her face tense, asked Boyd to walk her to the parking lot.

You sure you don't want me to drive you home in the truck? Boyd said. They were standing beside Lina's little car as she unlocked the door, threw her purse on the seat. Will Charlie get hired on at the yard again? she said. Her face was all angles and shadows in the moonlight.

No. Boyd jammed his cold hands into his jeans pockets.

Even with his new hand?

It's a hook, for God's sake. How's he gonna load ties with that?

Faint spurts of laughter came from the direction of the bar. Somewhere a door slammed. You wanna go get something to eat? said Boyd. Seems a little dumb standing in the cold like this.

In the truck they drove to a pizza place a few miles down the highway. Lina ordered a margarita, shook her hair out of its waitress ponytail. He was so excited when he left, she said. Kept talking about how he'd have two hands again.

You think you and Charlie'll get married? Boyd retrieved a piece of pepperoni, wiped sauce from his mouth.

I don't know. He hasn't asked me.

I'll tell you one thing. He's got good taste, my brother.

Lina put down the slice she was lifting to her mouth, said maybe she should go, she had work to do the next day. At the truck, opening the door for her, he tried tilting her face up to his but she stepped aside. Just take me back to the parking lot, okay, Boyd? He drove the narrow highway with the pedal pressed to the floor, flinging the truck round blind curves until she cried out and said would a kiss slow him down, would it? He pulled over then and held her long hair in his hands while he kissed her mouth, her throat. A car passed, washing them with its lights, and Boyd let her go and licked his lips, saying Jesus shakily. Jesus.

In the parking lot she jumped down without looking back, gunned the engine of the little car and roared away in a spray of gravel.

Charlie came home two weeks later with a silver hook connected to wires which ran over his shoulder to a battery pack. Twisted his shoulder to open and close the hook like a parrot's claw. He showed Boyd how he could undo zippers, peel eggs, brush his teeth. At the bar they began calling him Captain. He held a full tray of drinks in each hand now, raked the counter with his hook so that noisy drunks quietened down. Boyd found him lifting weights in his room, carrying a wheelbarrow full of old ties round the yard. Building up my muscles, was all he would say when Boyd asked him. I lost a lot of strength in my right arm.

Boyd was called out on an emergency crew, a derailment ten miles outside of Davis. Worked for two days pulling up twisted steel, broken glass, came home and slept, went out again and worked by the light of flares, the faces around him streaked with dirt, creosote burns across their shoulders. Sometime during that night Boyd turned and found the man at the other end of the steel beam was Charlie, grinning, his hook guiding the grapple into position. What the hell *you* doin here? Boyd shouted above the roar of the crane. Charlie shrugged, dodged the swinging beam, pulled the next into position. The foreman came by later, saw Charlie but didn't say anything. When a new crew member didn't see the steel above him swinging wildly, out of control, it was Charlie who leapt forward and pushed him to safety.

At the end of the night they drove home in the truck along the rutted back roads Charlie had somehow found in the dark. Charlie wiped his sweaty forehead against his upper arm, said I heard about you and Lina.

Boyd watched the headlights bounce off the trees, the blackness shredding into daylight. What did you hear?

That someone saw you. In the truck.

Charlie, it wasn't what you think.

You were sitting here, and she was sitting there, and there was this much space between you. Charlie held up his thumb and forefinger, pressed tight.

You're right. She damn near slapped my face.

Charlie rolled down the window and spat, pulled a cigarette package from his shirt pocket. Morning mist drifted in, thick and wet, made the hairs on Boyd's arms stand up. Charlie looked straight ahead, holding the truck steady over the ruts, cigarette trembling on his lower lip. In the smoke, the mist, the only clear thing was the hook, the rip it suddenly left in the seat between them.

In town Charlie parked in front of the hotel, said he needed breakfast but he had something else to do first. Boyd watched him walk down the street and round the corner, went inside and ordered ham and eggs. Waited five minutes, went outside and looked up and down the street. Walked round the corner to Second Avenue, past the warehouses, the railway depot, the barber shop in the old post office building. Charlie wasn't in one of the chairs, face white with lather, but a customer walking in carrying a parcel said, I just come from the freight office. Your brother's sure in a hell of a stew.

Boyd began to run. Down the street, across the grass median still slippery with frost under his boots, through the gravelled yard to the office. He could hear voices from a distance, shouting, a woman's scream. At the open door, his chest thudding, he saw a heaving mass of people, saw a couple of men in shirt-sleeves struggling with Charlie, saw Charlie break away and seize a chair and hurl it through the window. Saw Johnson grab Charlie's jacket, saw Charlie draw back and land a fist on his jaw, saw Johnson go down as two women fled shrieking past Boyd and the scream of a distant siren grew louder. He leapt over the counter, over Johnson motionless and bleeding on the floor, grabbed at his brother and felt the flesh open along his cheek as the hook swung at him. Charlie! For God's sake, Charlie! You gone completely crazy?

He crouched, circling, well out of range, watching his brother's face, distorted now into nothing he knew, into a mask of dirt and blood and sweat he couldn't read. Tell em, Boyd. The words were hissed from a white crack in the mask of dirt. Tell em I can lift steel, lay ties, use a spike hammer. Tell em you saw me.

He heard voices again behind him, saw the blue of police uniforms, a young sergeant he'd drunk with once or twice who nodded briefly at him. Charlie crumpled like the small boy who, dressed as a cowboy, had hidden in the barn, terrified by the painted faces of the older boys. He sat slumped in a chair as an officer handcuffed him and removed the prosthesis. Without the hook the stump in its padding looked shrunken, naked.

You're Boyd, aren't you? The young sergeant held the hook out, a gleaming question mark. You better get your brother home. Clean him up some. Behind them Johnson leaned white-faced on the counter, a woman dabbing at his cheek with paper towels. The sergeant motioned to the officer to remove the cuffs as Boyd stuffed the hook in his jacket. Rising to his feet, Charlie sagged against Boyd's shoulder, his shortened arm round Boyd's neck as together they moved towards the door.

THE EDGE OF THE WORLD

THE DAY AFTER the funeral Eva stood at the sink rinsing the dried husks of insects out of the ceiling shade from the living room. Outside the screen door, in the haze and dust of late summer, bees tumbled in the foxgloves bordering the porch where her brothers and sisters stood among their suitcases, fanning themselves with newspapers and talking in low voices. Should it be a marble headstone, or a granite one? Gothic lettering, or Old English? Eva, had she been asked, would have voted for a lilac bush at her mother's head instead of cold stone. But her brothers and sisters loomed above her as they had always done, not noticing her in the depths of their long shadows. She was surprised they had remembered, two weeks ago, to send a telegram summoning her home. She was still Evie, little Evie, pale and thin in her foreign clothes and oddly cropped hair. On the ladder of family opinion she occupied the bottom rung, below even Jim, who ought out of courtesy to be consulted though he sat speechless on the sofa, refusing to eat. This fact seemed to her more important than the character of the headstone, but only that morning her eldest sister had brought the untouched plate of eggs and bacon back to the kitchen and flung it in the garbage. And don't you go spoiling him when we leave, Evie, she said. He can't sit on that sofa forever.

This sister had been eighteen when her mother married Jim, twenty when Eva was born. They had long been used to the sound of their own voices, the smell of their own bodies, and when a tall big-knuckled man with a Nova Scotian accent moved in they had gone into a huddle from which they never quite emerged. All of them married and moved away as soon as possible, so that by the time Eva was six her ballet poses and her baton twirling took place under two pairs of eyes which never swerved from her pink tutu and dark pigtails. When they visited, trailing nieces and nephews not much younger than Eva, she came across them in corners whispering large words to her mother, unfamiliar names, until they all withdrew to a place of rolling hills and barns and white-faced cattle Eva had never seen, with the river that had drowned their father running through. When her mother grew ill, and then delirious, and became again a young farm wife in a checked apron, her sisters came home and took their place in her stories. In that world of memory Jim had no part, and by the time Eva arrived was refusing to enter his wife's room at all.

If she had lifted her head from the sink she might have seen the flutter of poplar leaves in the gully below the house, the way the clouds shadowed the snow-covered peaks in the distance. The same leaves fluttered, the same clouds shadowed the day she'd walked down the street all those centuries ago with her backpack and her airplane ticket. No one else seemed to wonder what lay beyond the mountains. Her high school classmates were too dazzled by their engagement rings to notice that distant shimmer beyond the edge of town. There, over the treetops – oh, look, look! – was the world, as enticing as a new coin. Twelve years later the houses had not stirred nor the people in them, the fireweed edging the roads still stiff with dust. The only change was that she now stood where her mother had stood, at the sink with her hands in water, while in the living room her father sat wrapped in a blanket, turning his dead wife's wedding ring over and over in his big hands.

When the taxi arrived her tall brothers heaved at the suitcases: We'll phone, we'll write, we'll be in touch, they said as they went down the steps. Her sisters, who had taken turns holding their mother's hand for the last three months, almost ran down the path. They were all going south, back to the weight of families, overflowing desks, the milky smell of living flesh. Eva, freshly plucked from her distant life, would be left in charge of the untouched plates, the silent house. With her brothers and sisters gone there would be no one left to talk at all.

Her father was standing at the living room window, blanket draped round his shoulders like a small boy playing Indians. Did you notice the horses in the garden this morning? he said.

Four white horses down there eating the lettuce. Your mother always liked horses. I must remember to tell her.

Eva went to the window and looked out. The lettuce patch was intact, the garden unmarked by hooves. The nearest farm was forty miles away. Her father still peered out into the garden as though the horses would gallop into view again at any moment. This was the longest speech he had made since Eva came home, said in the quiet firm way she remembered, and so she looked out the window again for a white muzzle to materialize, a dusty hoof. Saw only the vegetable patch her sisters had made a halfhearted attempt at weeding, the shed at the bottom of the garden, the pine tree with its frayed swing. What on earth was she thinking? Any visiting horses would have had to leap the hedge and would certainly have attracted the attention of the neighbours. Here they stood, the two of them, her father clutching the blanket in the hot sun at the window and she in the black tights and dress that were all she had thought to pack. There was solid ground between them, if only she could find it. Mom had horses when she was growing up, didn't she? she said.

Not like these ones, though. These were show horses. Pure white, with thick manes and tails. Her father paused, as if remembering. One of them had a black spot on its face. I noticed it because it was right by the window.

Beyond the hedge on her right Eva could see the broad back of the elderly German next door bending to adjust his sprinkler. A bird perched on a branch in the far corner of the garden. Hedges and human beings, that was what she saw, birds and sprinklers and sunlight on the lettuces. What, dear God, made those patterns resolve themselves in her father's eyes into prancing hooves and tossing manes? She wanted the ballast of her brothers and sisters, she wanted not to be alone with her father beside a window. I think you must have imagined them, Jim, she said. But he had moved back to the sofa where he sat down slowly and eased his legs onto a cushion. I'm very tired, Evie, he said. Very tired all of a sudden. I think I'll have a nap. Eva helped him spread the blanket over his legs and he smiled at her before turning his face to the back of the sofa.

In the evening Eva phoned her second sister. She could hear in the background the rise and hum of voices, a burst of music, a sudden shout, and her sister's voice threading it all together – the flight had been late, the children fretful, the kisses sticky, and the headstone, she now felt sure, should be onyx granite. Jim saw horses in the garden, after you left, said Eva. He's probably light-headed, said her sister, from lack of food. Has he eaten anything? A bit of stew? There you are, he ate something and he told you a story. Isn't that progress? Put in that light, Eva couldn't think why she'd been so oblivious. A scream echoed in her ear and her sister shouted, Stop it, Janine! I have to go, I'll call you next week.

After she hung up the phone Eva wandered in the darkening light from the kitchen to the hall to the back garden. She had forgotten the long evenings of northern summer, the apricot shading into turquoise above the mountains. Moths fluttered at the uncurtained windows. Upstairs her father slept, she hoped, dreaming of summers when she went with him and her mother to pick blueberries in the bush out the highway. In this light she could almost see the horses just beyond the hedge, out of sight, quietly cropping the long grass at the edge of the gully.

Only fourteen days ago she had walked down a street eight thousand miles away in the roar and tumble of a great city, had drunk tarry coffee at a Turkish café, had bought Canary Island tomatoes at a stand from a man whose lower lip dripped ash. In the shared flat six flights up with its clanking pipes and off-plumb doors they sat round the kitchen table eating chicken tikka and samosas from the Indian takeout downstairs, telling each other where to find cheap jeans, free meals, cut-price concert tickets, black-market televisions. In dim offices and grubby cafés they clerked and waited tables and typed and tended bar; they sold buttons, soap and china in the street markets; they could smell a bargain a mile away and spot a man with money at forty paces. They had all lived at different times on yogurt, canned beans, white bread and margarine. None of them could imagine silence, green grass, empty spaces; Eva woke up sweating sometimes from dreams in which she stood on a long and silent street stretching to the horizon, the direction of the city obscure. Now she worked as a receptionist in a small art gallery, she knew words like *painterly* and *spatial* and *linearity*, she would not ever again find herself trapped among people in steel-toed boots and lumberjack shirts who talked about catching their limit, pulling shifts, tipping a few after at the bar.

She had gone away to accumulate a different past. The world shook, oceans parted, elsewhere. She had thought, living in London and Paris and Madrid with her back turned, that the dust and the bush and the raw earth would fade and she would walk down the avenues in her fashionable shoes on her way to somewhere important. No one glittered on those streets where foxtail grew through the cracks in the sidewalk, where the drivers of pickup trucks stopped in the middle of the road to have conversations. Where the raw earth was churned up, houses thrown down carelessly, urgently, in the short northern summers. She had longed as a child for the glow of red brick, for the ornamental railings and fanlights and bay windows she had seen only in books. Now, living among brick grimed by the history of another country, she had only to touch it with her fingers to reassure herself it was her own.

She tried on books, cities, lovers, even a husband in a country where the word love, said in another language, seemed smaller, almost weightless. She learned to like young green wine, French cigarettes, black stockings, the crush of bodies everywhere, little cars on fast roads. Bare rooms were a virtue, as no one had any money to fill them, and reflected nothing. She forgot the smell of pine needles after rain, the taste of syrup and pancakes, even, during her marriage, the English words for sidewalk and window blind. After her marriage ended she cut her hair short, wore dark glasses, moved back to London, changed her name from Evelyn to Eva. In photographs, pale and thin, lipsticked and in black, it was clear that wherever she came from it was not from a fresh scar on the farthest edge of the New World.

In the morning Eva found an old pair of shorts that must have belonged to one of her sisters and mopped the kitchen floor while the vacuum cleaner stood expectantly in the upstairs hallway. Her flatmates would have been astonished to see her standing barelegged on that lake of linoleum, far from their overflowing ashtrays and wine-stained carpets. Clean sheets, folded linens, ordered plants in a row on the windowsill – that was what Eva had grown up with, and without them now she felt a kind of seasickness as though the house had shifted and lost its bearings. Her father had eaten half a piece of toast at breakfast and had even taken a few steps into the garden before complaining the sun was too bright. It's good to have you home, Evie, he had said. You know it's been a long time. He hadn't mentioned the horses. Grief, that was all it was, she had thought in the sunlight. It would pass, and she would be able to go home again in ten days to the tipsy flat, the stone-faced buildings. She had changed her return flight once already; she couldn't afford to pay the penalty fee again.

Upstairs the smell of mown grass drifted under the swelling curtains in her mother's bedroom. The bed had been freshly made before her sisters left, the night-table cleared of pills, her mother's clothes packed in boxes and taken to the thrift shop. No sign that a woman with a pale face and thinning hair had lain here for months, barely noticing that Eva had come home. From the window Eva could see across the gully to the belt of forest and the dusty blur of mining road up the mountain. Evie! she heard, and then again: Evie! She ran downstairs. Her father clutched a corner of the blanket to his chest. I thought I heard footsteps, Evie. Upstairs in your mother's room. His face was drawn taut, his mouth turned upside down, masklike.

It was me, Jim. Just me. I went in to close the window.

I could of sworn.... His eyes drifted from her face to a point just beyond her shoulder to the living room window. She had a very light step, you know. Very distinctive. I could of sworn it was her.

Maybe you'd like to have a nap, Jim. Do you think? An afternoon nap?

She was repeating things, as if to a child: a nap, a nice nap, a nap for Jim. Twelve years ago she'd left a man with the corded arms and neck of someone who'd done physical work all his life; now the skin at his throat was wattled and coarse. She would make something tempting, a pie perhaps, though she'd never made pastry in her life. She found an old recipe book of her mother's, picked overgrown rhubarb from the garden, measured and chopped and mixed in the wilting kitchen. At dinner Jim ate half a pork chop and almost finished a second piece of pie. Afterwards they sat out in the garden with their coffees, even though he needed a second blanket, and talked about a trip they'd made once to Vancouver when Eva was eleven. He answered when spoken to, paused in the right places, even laughed once or twice. Fresh air and good food and time; her brothers and sisters were right, that was all he needed.

Do you remember I taught you how to play gin rummy? her father said the following morning. She had come downstairs early to find him standing at the window in his pyjamas, so absorbed he didn't see her until she said his name. I was watching, he said – dear God, not the horses again, not – how the swallows skim over the grass in the morning. Did you ever notice? Some muscle in her stomach unclenched. All I can see from my flat window, she said, is traffic. And people.

All that noise, her father said. Imagine. Even at breakfast. I think I might be able to manage a boiled egg this morning, Evie.

She cooked two boiled eggs and mashed them in a bowl so he couldn't tell. At four years old this had been her favourite breakfast, with bread soldiers ranged round her plate. Her father ate everything, asked for more coffee, and mentioned the gin rummy, did she remember? You sat at that end of the table – he pointed – holding the cards like a pro. Your mother said what was I thinking of, teaching you to gamble. And I said I was teaching you how not to get cheated.

She did remember. She had sat where she sat now in her kimono, her sandalled feet dangling below the chair, and stared at the kings and queens with their pointed chins and sly faces while words collided in the air above her head. Card games. At *her* age. What was he thinking of? Might as well learn now, mightn't she? You like it, don't you, sweetie? She sure has an aptitude. They had played in the gathering dusk until bedtime while her mother's disapproval bore down on them like a cold front from the living room.

How about a game, Evie? If I can find a pack of cards. I think your mother might have got rid of them all.

They found a pack in one of the kitchen drawers, buried under carefully rolled lengths of string and half-spent candles. The cards flew and snapped between her father's thick fingers as he shuffled and dealt. Eva had lost ten dollars by the time the doorbell rang at eleven-fifteen: a delivery van with flowers from a second cousin in Saskatchewan who'd just heard. Eva laid the crackling cellophane on the breakfast table among the hardened plates while she filled a vase with water. When she returned her father was holding the gift card and wiping his eyes with a napkin.

I shouldn't of done that, Evie. I shouldn't of forgot myself like that.

Like what, Jim?

Sitting here in the middle of the day playing cards like that. Having a good time just after your mother – He stopped and blew his nose into the napkin. I'm giving you back what I won, Evie. I'm going to rest up a bit.

Eva did the laundry, ate lunch alone, went out for groceries while her father slept on the sofa. When she came back he was standing by the telephone, hair askew. I was looking up my friend Jack's number, he said as Eva put the grocery bag on the counter. Haven't heard from Jack in a long while.

There had been a Jack Apsey who had served with Jim during the war, but he had died while Eva was in her teens. Perhaps someone named Jack had called? I don't know who you mean, Jim, she said, the can of asparagus pausing in mid-air.

Jack, you know. My good buddy Jack. Her father's voice shook with annoyance and he flung a hand in her direction. We saw action together. Normandy. Drinking cognac. Jack knew some French, you know. *Garçon*, he kept saying. *Garçon! Plus de cognac!* Her father laughed deep in his throat, shivered and tightened his blanket. Funniest damn thing, you know, Evie, but I can't remember the number.

As soon as I unpack the groceries, Jim. I'll try and get it for you. Now you go and relax.

Once he was safely in the living room she called the doctor's office. Would she hold on while they checked his file?

He'd had a prescription for a mild tranquillizer a month ago, would she like to have it refilled? He's not eating properly, said Eva. He's imagining things. He's had a shock, said the smooth professional voice at the other end. It's quite a common reaction after a spouse dies. But if you'd like an appointment.... No, said Eva, no, thank you, and hung up. What would she say? That he'd talked, once, about a memory of horses; that there'd been a moment of confusion about a dead army buddy? Tiny slippages in the midst of the darkness he'd entered, sitting on that sofa day after day while upstairs his wife passed from flesh into transparency. An image of the city, its evening spark and tingle, rose before her and on impulse she dialled the flat, but there was no answer.

After supper her brother phoned, the one who had waved from the taxi window. You didn't call this morning, did you? said Eva. Jim was standing by the phone when I got back from shopping, I thought maybe – Two eggs, at breakfast. And a bit of fish for dinner. And chocolate pudding.

There you go, then, said her brother, and talked of backlogged paperwork, a leaking roof, the cost of new skates and gymnastics lessons, here he was still at work at eight o'clock and sometimes his brain felt as if it wouldn't hold another single thought. Someone with a name like Jack must have called, said Eva. He kept talking about his army buddy, the one who died. Wanting to phone him. Did you know he saw horses outside the living room window, the morning you left? White show horses? That's what you all keep saying, but how much time is more time?

Her brother spoke of not being able to concentrate, of seeing their mother's face superimposed over the papers on his desk, floating on the wall above his calendar. Pointed out that it wasn't such a leap to illusory horses and ghostly men, just grief taking a different shape. They were very close, you know, Evie. Went for a walk every night down the avenue, holding hands. You've been away a long time, you don't remember.

What she remembered were the brittle silences that lasted for days while she tiptoed back and forth like an ambassador between warring countries. Her brothers and sisters had left home by then – was that when the temperature changed?

When the peace offerings of flowers lay shredded on the kitchen floor, followed by thaws during which her father was permitted to re-enter the dining room, the kitchen, the bedroom? Later on, her father's slow retreat into the basement – a ham radio, a stamp collection – while she danced ever faster in her ballet shoes, twirled her baton ever more vigorously to draw the enemy fire. Had all that really changed after she left, or had her brothers and sisters unveiled a pastel watercolour in which her parents strolled forever down an impossibly sunny avenue?

I have ten days, said Eva, before my flight home. I have paperwork and messages waiting on my desk too. Suppose he isn't better? What then?

Two days ago he wasn't eating, said her brother, let alone talking. That's dramatic improvement in my book. You're doing wonders for him, Evie. He spoke of sharing the burden, shouldering the load, lending a hand, pitching in. Of how they were all exhausted, wrung out by grief, they had nothing left, it was only fair that she took her turn with someone who, after all, wasn't dying. Who needed his daughter. What if you had to stay for a couple more weeks? he said. Would that be too much to ask, after twelve years?

I have, said Eva, a life. Going on in the city without me. I can't stay, any more than you can. If she were there now she would be leaning beside the evening river watching the slow igniting of the towers on the opposite bank, except that the river seemed to be ebbing, leaving behind a dust-coloured verge of fireweed, while before her the pillars of light changed into a wall of forest. That was what they wanted, her brothers and sisters – they wanted her to stay and mop and dust and bake, to stoke the fires and sweep the hearth, to answer their phone calls a year or five years or ten from now saying Jim was fine and had taken a little custard, and later still to say oh, so sad, he'd passed away just that morning, she'd taken the spade and buried him under the pine tree. By that time she would have widened and solidified, let her hair grow, she would stand with her arms buried up to the elbows in flour every morning and listen to news reports about the world of the cities. After all, she had made no commitments, had taken no hostages. She could live her tumbleweed life here as well as anywhere else.

I was told not to spoil him, said Eva. You all said he'd snap out of it, you went off and talked about marble and what the lettering should be. I don't care if it's granite or marble or a big neon sign, and she hung up.

The next afternoon Jim went for a long walk by himself, talked about the leaves already changing colour when he came back, ate potatoes and ham and baked beans for supper and asked for more. On the strength of that second helping Eva phoned the flat to let them know she'd be home in a week, hoping to catch someone coming in from a Friday night out. A voice she didn't recognize answered on the tenth ring, barely audible over the music and loud voices in the background. Moira? Moira who? Lived there, did she? The owner of the voice hadn't met her but supposed she might be the host of the party. Spur-of-the-moment thing really, because Johnny – didn't she know Johnny? Everyone knew Johnny – was getting married. Wonderful party, what a shame she was missing it, the police had already been round twice. Hang on half a mo, she'd go and see if she could find Moira. There was a loud clunk and then a series of diminishing thuds as though the phone had been left to dangle from its wall bracket. Dammit anyway – hadn't Moira remembered about the threatened eviction notice after the last party? And where was Suzy? Eva banged the phone down.

In the morning Jim was flushed and restless and refused to get up. There was a nasty strain of summer flu going round, the doctor's office said, he needed rest and plenty of fluids. Eva ran up and down stairs with icepacks and orange juice, brandy and soup. By the following evening he seemed better, if rather weak, but Eva herself had a sore throat and a wobbliness in her knees. She spent two nights and a day in bed. She heard Jim moving about occasionally, heard a door shut or the toilet flush, but mostly she slept. Late on the second evening, still damp with fever, she tried phoning the flat again. Eight hours ahead, seven in the morning, but still there was no answer.

She saw the black shoulders of the phone in the flat's tiny kitchen, heard its shrill double ring, saw herself running to answer it. After twelve rings she hung up. They were out already among the hum and energy and the little darting cars, while she sat with her unwashed skin in a crumpled night-gown in a house that might as well be empty.

She must have slept again, because she awoke out of a sticky and fitful sleep and heard music downstairs. Had her father turned the radio on, for the first time in weeks? She sat up slowly; she was dizzy for lack of food. She put on her robe and went slowly downstairs, holding on to the banister. Four steps from the bottom, overlooking the living room, she halted. Under blazing lights, to the strains of a Strauss waltz on the record player, her father was circling the floor in grace-ful arcs, his arms in partnering position, completely naked. His head erect, arms poised, he might have been in a formal ballroom among tuxedoed men and bejewelled women, his feet travelling a pattern they hadn't followed in forty years. On his second sweep past the stairs he looked up at Eva and nod-ded, smiling, as though to a fellow guest. Eva stepped deliber-ately into his path but he waltzed nimbly around her, twitch-ing imaginary coattails out of the way. Outside, beyond the naked panes of glass, he waltzed just as easily over the dark and dewy lawn, twirling past the pine tree and the compost heap in full view of the neighbourhood. Eva snapped the drapes shut and turned off the record player, and Jim came to a bewildered and uncertain stop.

What did you do that for? he said. We were having a lovely time.

You haven't got any clothes on, Jim, she said, though she was the one shivering. You're going to get cold.

I was dancing, Evie. That was all. I haven't danced with your mother in such a long time. He moved towards the sofa and groped for its back as he sat down slowly.

It's late, Jim. You should be in bed. Eva draped the blanket round his shoulders and retrieved his slippers from the far side of the room. Her body shook and her stomach felt cramped and nauseous. Let's go upstairs and tuck you in.

But I want to dance with your mother again. Under the blanket she saw how thin he'd become, the long stringy tendons in his thighs. She loved waltzing, you know. I'd almost forgotten how. We circled round and round and round for hours. The bright lights made her eyes water, the pattern on the carpet vibrated. She sat on the sofa next to her father and tried to control the rising nausea. Round and round and round, he said. It all came back in a rush. After all these years.

She had to get him upstairs while she still had the strength. She started to rise but he pulled at her arm. Let me stay for a while, Evie. Please. It's been such a long time.

And what was the harm, she thought? He had looked gay, smiling, energetic. Perhaps, if he put his pyjamas on, she should just let him stay and dance while she went back to bed. What was the harm in that?

I want to dance till dawn, Evie. He had leaned towards her and spoke in a lowered voice, as though sharing a secret. That's when the horses come to the window. I don't want to miss them.

Behind his uncombed head the light shone like a halo. Eva closed her eyes and only with great effort opened them again. Her father was going somewhere she could not follow, slipping beyond her reach, though she wanted desperately to call him back. Her head throbbed, her limbs felt like ice. She leaned her head against his shoulder and he patted her hand. Aren't you feeling well, Evie? You should go to bed, you know. Get some rest. He lifted his arm so that the blanket fell around her and she lay unresisting against his melting flesh, his cheek resting on the top of her head.

PRETTY BANGS

SIMON STOOD at the counter in the basement with a tin of potassium nitrate in one hand and a half-eaten sandwich in the other. Around him the empty house expanded in accommodating silence, waiting, listening. The book lay open nearby, several pages burnt through where he'd leaned too close to the Bunsen burner. He measured the nitrate into a beaker with one of his mother's tablespoons and added sulphur and charcoal. The book didn't mention potassium chlorate but he added a tablespoon anyway; the results with nitrate alone had been disappointing.

From under the counter he took the rocket, smoothing the aluminum foil over its cardboard heart. He stuffed a crumpled piece of newspaper in one end, lifted the nose-cone and poured in the greyish-yellow mixture from the beaker. The familiar sting of the sulphur in his nostrils quickened him. He tamped the mixture down with more newspaper, replaced the nose-cone and opened the basement door. It had stopped raining but the eaves still dripped.

The guttering was hidden under the hedge. He laid it against the base of the patio table at a sixty-degree angle, hoping his father hadn't noticed the burn marks on the flagstones. 'Please,' he said softly as he placed the rocket in the guttering. 'Please.' He took matches from his pocket and lit the newspaper. A flash of orange flame, a puff of smoke, a loud bang. The rocket quivered and lay still.

Simon gave one of the patio chairs a kick that landed it inches from the French windows. If only he knew someone he could ask, an aeronautical engineer for example. After long searching he'd found the formula he needed in a thin red book wedged between two dusty chemistry texts in a secondhand bookstore. *Experiments for the Serious Amateur Chemist*, written by a Mr. Baxter Griff and published in 1949. Mr. Griff pulled no punches. There were instructions for making smoke bombs, 'in your own backyard', how to generate enough heat to melt glass, and, at last, how to make gunpowder. Mr. Griff himself occupied the frontispiece, earnest in horn-rimmed glasses and a white smock. Simon carried the book home under his jacket and read it beneath the covers with a flashlight. His classmates were content to watch their teacher produce serpents' eggs and invisible ink; wait till they saw a blastoff!

But after nineteen fruitless attempts there was clearly something wrong with the rocket fuel. Unless, of course, Mr. Griff promised more than he delivered, and had neglected to mention a key ingredient. On the other hand it had been his own idea to use the gunpowder to launch a rocket. He dug in his pockets for the cigarette stub he'd saved. At school they'd had a talk on the dangers of smoking by a man from the Red Cross who'd brought a cross-section of lung, brown and papery. Simon looked closely at the jar when it reached his desk. Bark, obviously, shaved paper thin. He inhaled more deeply.

It was cold and getting dark, and his mother would be home soon. He would have to show her the report card. He pinched out the cigarette, put the guttering away and carried the rocket inside. On a sheet of paper taped to the wall beside the counter, under the previous entry, he wrote the date and, in neat capital letters, 'Negative. Liftoff nil.'

He'd been given the chemistry set as a birthday present by his Uncle Neville. His uncle's presents were like no one else's; there'd been a painted wooden bird once that flew around the room, and an old-fashioned train engine, belching real steam. He hadn't known he wanted a chemistry set, but when he opened the lid and saw the glass test tubes, the vials of blue and pink and copper powders, the little weighing scale, his fingers tingled. 'Try not to envelop us in clouds of smoke before dinner, Simon,' said his father. 'I think Neville's forgotten what it's like to be eleven.'

'Twelve,' said Simon, his cheeks a mortifying pink, and opened a package from his parents which turned out to be a boxed scarf and glove set. 'If Simon blew the roof off,' said his brother Jeff, 'would we have a case against Uncle Neville?'

'An interesting question in tort law.' His father placed his fingertips together. 'I rather think a judge might find in our favour. But fortunately for Neville, I don't believe in litigation within families.'

'Or within law firms,' said Simon before he knew what he was going to say. Both his father and his uncle were senior partners in the law firm founded by his grandfather, who had gone on to become a provincial Supreme Court judge.

'Don't be cheeky, Simon,' said his mother. 'Do those gloves fit?'

'Then *I* could sue Simon instead,' said Jeff, 'at least once I reach my majority.' Jeff was planning to take law at Osgoode and then enter the family firm. Suits, countersuits, rollovers, undertakings – what life did that have compared to these vials of lycopodium powder and antimony sulfide?

When the door opened at ten after six Simon was standing in the kitchen mixing his mother's favourite drink, his own invention of white rum, dry sherry and pineapple juice. His mother came in unbuttoning her raincoat and kissed him. 'Simon, you angel. How did you know I'd need this?'

'Adult brain chemistry. Malfunctions without C_2H_5 and fruit sugar.'

'As long as it's alcoholic.' She leaned against the dishwasher, holding the glass. 'You haven't grown another inch, have you? Stand straight.' She drew her hand across his dark cropped hair to her forehead.

'We're almost even, Mom.'

'Then you *have*. What does that make you, five six and a half?'

'Five seven.'

'That's it, sorry. No enchiladas for you tonight.'

'Yuck. I'd rather have a peanut butter sandwich anyway.'

'You have to have *something* else, Simon. Peanut butter isn't – well, *balanced*.'

'Seventeen milligrams of calcium, ninety-two milligrams of phosphorus, and a hundred and fifty-one milligrams of potassium, per ounce.' Simon stuck his thumbs through the beltloops of his jeans.

'I suppose you know how many grams of calcium it takes to produce a one-inch growth spurt.'

'A lot more than I'm getting around here. This, on the other hand –' He picked up her drink and took a swig. His mother snatched the glass away. 'I think you're getting too old to be making these on your own. Hand me the salad spinner, would you? Did your father phone?'

'Yes to número uno and no to número dos.' Simon walked his fingers along the counter edge and spun in a circle before opening the cupboard door.

'And don't show off.'

'I'm not showing off. We learned that months ago in Spanish class.'

'I didn't know you were taking Spanish.' Two small parallel grooves appeared between his mother's eyebrows as she rinsed the lettuce.

'Sí, mamá. Estoy muy contento con mi clase de español.'

She smiled at him. 'All these hidden talents! A good nose, a good ear – where do you get them?'

'The trouble is, they don't count for very much at school.'

'Didn't you get your report card today?'

'I think you'd better finish your drink first,' said Simon.

The phone rang. It wasn't his father but Jeff, saying he was staying for supper at Aaron's. Simon watched his mother pick up his report card from the hall table and listened to Jeff saying something about lacrosse practice. 'I'm going to the hardware store for a new beaker,' he called when he hung up, and left through the patio windows without his jacket.

He crept back an hour later and stood in the hallway, shivering. He could hear his mother's voice indistinctly through the closed kitchen door. Talking on the phone to his father, no doubt. In the darkened basement he stood still until his breathing slowed, then gently lifted the receiver of the extension phone that his father had had installed three years ago during a burst of enthusiasm for carpentry.

'It wasn't raining,' his mother was saying. 'Not that afternoon. In the morning, but not in the afternoon.'

'But I got wet,' said his father. 'I was pushing Simon in the stroller, and I remember picking him up and my jacket was quite wet.'

'We walked to where the seawall ended then. And you carried the stroller up a grassy bank – I had Simon – and you slipped and put an arm through the stroller, and we laughed and laughed. It was such a long time since we'd laughed.'

'We had tea at a tea-shop on Denman Street. And Simon had a dish of ice cream, but he wouldn't let me feed him. He said he was a big boy and took the spoon out of my hand.'

'Well, he didn't know you.'

'Oh, I don't think it was that. He wanted to be grown up.'

'Yes, but he wanted a father too. That night he kept asking me if you were going to be his daddy.'

The Bunsen burner, the beakers, the coloured powders shrivelled and receded and left Simon floating in a vast darkness.

'It was a shock, seeing you standing at the bus stop holding that small dark-haired boy,' his father said. 'After – well, it was more than two years then, wasn't it? I knew he wouldn't look like me, but it's funny, I was glad he didn't look like you either. Because then he would be yours all the time, or *his*, but never mine.'

'The twelfth of November. Ten years ago today,' said his mother. 'And so mild, I don't think we've had such a mild November since. I only had on a light jacket, that grey wool suit. I wore it deliberately, it had been my going-away outfit when we got married, did you remember? I must have already decided.'

'Had you?'

'Oh yes, I think so. Simon needed a father, and –'

'A father. Any old father.'

'I didn't mean it like that. A caring father. The way you were with Jeff, before we separated. But it wasn't till I saw you together with him that day that I thought: yes. This might work.'

'So I passed some sort of test?'

'You make it sound as though everything can be separated out into pieces.'

'I was *trained* to do that, to separate emotion from fact.' His father's voice rose.

After a pause his mother said, 'It was a mutual decision, getting back together.'

'Was it? Is there ever, really, such a thing as a mutual decision?'

'A decision was made.' His mother's voice was weary,
unyielding. 'Will you be home late?'

'Around ten.'

The phone clicked. Simon put a foot out in the floating
darkness and found that the floor had not dissolved into
vapour. Mr. Griff hadn't mentioned this ability of solids to
shift into fluid state. He picked up the book with cramped
fingers and sat curled over it, listening to Mr. Griff describe
the properties of phosphorus in a voice that faded in and out of
those others that beat in his blood.

'I won't show your father the report card, this time,' said his
mother in the morning, snapping her briefcase shut. 'That'll
give you another semester to pull up your marks.'

'Mmm,' said Simon. He was eating a piece of toast and pulling a sweater over his head at the same time.

'Your father wouldn't understand why you're getting C's in
chemistry and math when last year you were getting A's.'

Simon straightened his sweater and ran his fingers through
his hair.

'There must be something you haven't told me. Some problem at school or something. Should I talk to your teacher?'

'No.' Even without looking he could see her face with those
two short parallel lines just above her nose. He stared out the
window and levered a toast crumb out of a back tooth with his
tongue.

'Are they giving you too much homework?'

'No.' Being an adult sometimes seemed like a licence to ask
questions that any intelligent child would think beneath con-
tempt. 'I'm bored, that's all.'

'But it should all be easy for you, Simon. Jeff's the one who
has to work to keep his marks up.' She lifted her briefcase off
the counter. 'Can you remember to put the casserole in at
five? I won't be home till seven. And don't forget it's your
father's birthday on Friday.'

The door slammed. The sound of her car starting up filled

the living room as Simon lay on the couch, carving a tiny crosshatching on the walnut coffee table with his penknife.

When he got home from school it was raining hard. He made up the gunpowder mixture anyway and assembled his launching pad under the patio overhang, trying to light the newspaper with matches that kept going out. At last a match held and the paper crackled into flame. He clenched his fists as it burnt to crumpling ash and went out. Perhaps the powder had got damp. He was chilled and shivering; his jacket was still wet from the walk home. He stood with his hands in his pockets and looked up at the grey weight of sky. The trees at the bottom of the garden were a blur through the rain. He picked up the rocket and went inside. Negative, he wrote for the twentieth time on the sheet of paper. Aiming for the moon, he had fallen on his face, and perhaps Mr. Griff was trying to tell him something. He could not yet make rockets fly, Mr. Griff seemed to be saying, but he could make gunpowder, and the book had a whole chapter on fireworks. Perhaps, if he followed instructions to the letter, he could at least fill the night sky with stars. And he could follow in the footsteps of Uncle Neville and give his father something really different for his birthday. He rubbed his numbed fingers together, whistling as he began writing down a list of ingredients.

He talked Jeff into driving him out to the chemical supply store in Richmond, where they wouldn't sell to anyone under sixteen, by promising to take over Jeff's leaf-raking duties that weekend. While they drove Simon looked out the window at the flat farmland and formed questions in his head, even cleared his throat once or twice. Did Jeff remember a time when his father wasn't there, a time when another man picked him up and called him sonny? A day during that time when his mother brought home a new baby brother? Half-brother, but would she have said that to a four-year-old? Or had she told him later and made him promise not to tell? And what had happened to the man who had played pat-a-cake with Jeff but had left Simon nothing, not even his name?

'You got a frog in your throat?' said Jeff.

'Did mom and dad have – ?' he said, but Jeff had swung right into the parking lot of the supply store and jerked to a stop. 'And don't take all day,' Jeff said as they walked towards the door.

After dinner that evening he cut fencing wire into foot-long lengths to make sparklers. He coated half of each length with a mixture of gum arabic and gunpowder, taking care to get the coating even. He also made the touch paper, soaking several sheets of filter paper in potassium nitrate solution and hanging them up to dry.

The next day, Thursday, he borrowed his father's unused electric drill to make a hole in the base of one of his mother's brass flowerpots. He threaded a strip of touch paper through the hole and filled the pot with a mixture of powdered zinc, magnesium, iron, and gunpowder. On Friday morning he got up early to grind the crystals for the coloured fires; Mr. Griff had explained that this was best left to last. After school he piled all his supplies against the basement door and eyed the clouds. It had been overcast all day but so far the rain had held off. His father was coming home early for once, and before the coffee and cake in the living room he would spring his surprise.

While his mother and Jeff loaded the plates in the dishwasher, he carried the fireworks outside one by one and stacked them behind the patio wall. His father had wanted an explanation, and for once Jeff had said Simon could refuse to answer by taking Section 11(c) against self-incrimination. It had turned into a fine night, starry and cold. He picked a spot on the lawn about twenty-five feet from the window as his launch site, then went inside to switch off the living room lights and check the sight-lines. When he turned to whistle a summons Jeff had joined his father at the dining room table, their blond heads bent together over the crossword puzzle.

From outside he watched them come into the living room, his father holding his newspaper, Jeff feinting at an imaginary opponent, his mother with his father's jacket draped over her shoulders. He placed one of the coloured fires on the launch site and dropped three matches before he managed to light one, his fingers clumsy in gloves. The powder caught and exploded in a roof-high shower of brilliant yellow light. If he couldn't yet have the moon he could have stars, leaping out of his own hands, summoned from a dark basement for their moment of life.

He kicked away the metal container, still sputtering, and lit another, in an explosion of pink rain. A third went up in arrows of blue and orange. The last, a double-quantity multicoloured, filled the air with the sickly smell of burning spices as white and green and purple comets showered the house. He hoped Mr. Griff knew what he was doing; the hose was stored inside for the winter. But already the stars were fading, and he manoeuvred the heavy flowerpot into place.

The touch paper went out the first time he tried to light it; perhaps it had got damp. He jiggled it to loosen the powder and swore softly under his breath. He sensed rather than saw the dark figures pinned to the windowpane; 'Don't let me down now, Mr. Griff,' he said out loud. With chilled fingers he lit another match. The touch paper caught, held, and a flower petal shape burst high in the air, now pink, now blue, now gold, now a budlike cluster, now blossoming above the roof. A spectacle worthy of the emperors of China, Mr. Griff had claimed, and had not disappointed. Perhaps he would go to China and become fireworks maker to the emperor. As the gold and silver stars rained around him he saw his mother's smiling face, her palms on the glass, and Jeff with his nose pressed to the window, his father standing behind them, face half in shadow. The firework exploded in a final rainbow shower and died away. In the darkness, the after-image of the stars still lingering, he made a low and elaborate bow.

His mother met him at the kitchen doorway as he was pulling off his gloves. 'Sweetheart, that was wonderful! Did you do all that yourself? I wasn't sure when they landed on the roof, but they're really quite harmless, aren't they?' While she arranged cups and plates on a tray, he stuck the sparklers in the birthday cake and lit a match. They stood for a moment in the darkened dining room with the blazing cake between them until his mother lifted up the tray and said, 'One, two, three.' Singing as they went into the living room, his voice cracking slightly under her higher one.

As the cake was lowered onto the coffee table his father folded his newspaper and raised his eyebrows, smiling. 'Do we owe this drama to Simon too?' he said. The tops of the sparklers twisted and curled downwards in thin threads.

'At least you don't have to use any breath on this one.' His mother was laughing as she sliced cake.

'Just as well, at my age,' said his father, accepting a plate. 'Forty-six. Incomprehensible.'

'Smasheroo cake, Mom,' said Jeff, forking in half his piece at once. His father said, 'Now where did you pick all that up? You haven't been practising down there in the basement, I hope.'

'I haven't been practising at all,' said Simon.

'You want us to believe you just invented those fireworks?'

'No. I used a book.' Would his father demand to see it? 'I followed the instructions.'

'Sounds a bit dangerous to me.'

'I know what I'm doing,' Simon said. And because that sounded bald, rude, 'I've worked my way up from simple experiments. I'm very careful.'

'It was a wonderful show, darling,' said his mother.

'I'd be happier if you'd turn your obvious talents to a less dramatic line of inquiry,' his father said. 'But it was quite a show for an amateur, son. Not much future in it, but very clever.'

Simon shook his head at the plate his mother held out to him. For the second time that evening his father looked surprised. 'Aren't you having any birthday cake?'

'No,' said Simon, and stood up. 'I'm going to go and practise making something with more future in it. Like dynamite.'

'Simon!' said his mother, but Simon had already reached the stairs.

In the basement he fed the pages of Mr. Griff's book one by one into the flame of the Bunsen burner and understood that he had been deceived. Pretty bangs, that was what he was being allowed to do – stars and flowers that fell harmlessly around the garden. All he had to show for the rocket were burn marks on the patio.

The pale blue flame flickered like a tongue round Mr. Griff's glasses. If he could not make, he would steal: the contents of rifle cartridges, blasting caps, grenades from the military museum. That would have to do until he grew up and found all the adult world laid open before him. The rocket blasted upwards, its orange tail pulsating, leaving his father open-mouthed at the window and a wide black scar across the lawn.

ROOFTOP DANCING

THE DAY HER BROTHER killed himself, Maureen Logan
spent the morning on a step-ladder in her kitchen, peering up
at the ceiling through paint-flecked eyelashes while three
thousand miles away, on the roof of his apartment building,
Richard contemplated his moment of flight. She must have
been looking upward even as he looked down, and if it hadn't
been for a moment's distraction – a sound in the street, perhaps – she was sure their gazes would have met. Richie! she
would have called to the figure in the leather jacket, as if he
were a small boy again and she the older sister holding out her
arms. But something intervened, she had turned her head, and
when she looked back at the ceiling all she saw was paint.

It was her brother Edward who phoned. Maureen clutched
the receiver as though drowning; the paint trays, the drop
sheets, the neat trim of masking tape faded like breath.
Edward's voice was ridiculously substantial. It broke only
once, like a teenager's, when he said There's no easy way to
tell you this, Maureen, and she felt an intense and tender pity,
not for Richard who was beyond it but for Edward, that he had
to endure the words coming out of his mouth. It was Edward,
twelve years ago, who had phoned when their father died, and
at their mother's over the following week she had watched
him covertly, sure that as the messenger he bore some new
and indelible mark of sorrow.

At six this morning, said Edward, somebody coming home
from a party found him. Because he was listed as next of kin,
he supposed – a police officer had come to the door an hour
ago. No, he hadn't phoned Mom yet. No, they didn't think it
was an accident. Why, Maureen, in God's name why? How do
you tell a nine-year-old his uncle jumped off a building? They
could wait for the colour photographs or go to Vancouver to
identify the body. He had a flight out of Calgary in two hours.
You can't be there alone, Maureen had said. I want to go. Yes,
I'm sure. Can you book me a room there too? Her obedient

hand picked up a pen and formed words with firm and steady letters, though the phone on her shoulder shook.

After she hung up Maureen crouched on the floor, hugging her stomach. A faint grey vapour seemed to leak from the walls, blotting out colour and shape. She began to rock, backwards and forwards – there were images out there, waiting at the edge of the vapour, and she wanted to keep them at a distance. Martin, for example, who rose from what had been his favourite chair and came towards her. He hadn't sat in that chair for three years but he rose from it several times, vanishing before he reached her. She wanted Martin in the flesh to bend over her, call her Reenie again, stroke the back of her neck, but that Martin lived another life in another city, having left no evidence of their five years together.

She pushed herself off the floor and discovered she was shaking. In the kitchen she held her hands over the gas flame, even lowered a palm, but though she saw the red welt rising she felt nothing. She turned with the kettle in her hand and said Damn you to the figure on the motor-bike in his leather jacket, laughing, shaking his hair out of his eyes. A boy, always, though he would have been thirty in four months. Always would be nearly thirty, now. There was that slight hump in his nose where he'd broken it, falling out of a tree at ten. At twelve, falling out of the same tree, he'd broken an arm and his left leg. But had picked himself up and hopped to the kitchen door, still grinning, to tell their mother.

She poured boiling water into a teapot, filled a mug, drank. She would not feel. Look, her hand holding the mug was steady. Her mind was like some small scrambling animal borne away by flood and seizing at twigs. There would be a faint snaky river where she'd left off painting. She'd gone to three paint stores to find that shade of yellow, debating over custard and lemon, freesia and buttercup, while Richard walked the streets of Vancouver measuring himself against the heights of buildings. Too much blue, she'd said to the sales clerks, too little orange, while Richard gazed at the guns in the sporting goods store, the cool rows of pills in the pharmacy. Counted the steps up to the rooftop while she ascended and descended her ladder, dipping the roller into fresh paint. If only he'd come crashing through her ceiling, had stood amid shattered timbers dusting himself off – she would have kissed him on his warm mouth and told him to be more careful in future.

Richard. Oh Richard. The small animal thrashed around for another twig. Rinse out the mug, fill a jar with paint thinner and put the brushes in. The step-ladder would stand waiting for her until she got back. Got back from what? Impossible to imagine anything on the other side of where she was now going. Practical. Not feel. She was always practical, calm, level-headed; people told her that. Phones, flights, clean underwear – she was good at those kinds of things. She would phone, she would fly, she would take clean underwear and dark glasses, and in this dying month of November she would hold the rippling centre of the world steady.

You said the airport, isn't it, Mrs? said the cab driver, and she struggled out of a great fog to say yes. On the slushy streets two raw-cheeked toddlers with identical blue toques went by in a stroller. Three men holding briefcases stood linked by a cloud of breath under a lamppost. Several teenage girls bubbled out of a mall, chattering soundlessly, tugging sleeves down over their bare hands. On this dirty dull ordinary late Saturday afternoon they moved as though underwater through the exhaust and the car horns and the neon, their faces full of energy and knowledge and secrets and hopes and lies. They hadn't left behind a jagged line on a ceiling, rushing to another city in paint-spattered jeans as though someone were dying and not dead. She breathed on the cold glass and the teenagers disappeared.

Temperature must be dropping, the cabbie said. Getting very slippery. Perhaps they'd slide into another car, gently of course, nobody hurt, but she'd miss her plane and go home to bed, start the day over with tea and toast and getting ready to paint and no call from Edward at all. No, a call instead from Martin, in town unexpectedly and was she free for lunch, and they'd go for a walk after in the park and watch the ducks swimming in their little holes in the ice – Bloody idiot! She jumped. The cabbie had rolled down his window and was yelling at the driver in the next lane. What do you think you are doing, cutting me off like that? You call that driving? I take your licence number – what? I rather be that than a bloody stupid driver!

Here was a twig, a solid branch in fact, but she didn't want it. Those raised voices, those waving hands, all that noise and movement scattered in spendthrift handfuls over the dirty snow. In a world of dead brothers, she wanted to say, tread softly and lower your voices. Another animal, clawed and fanged, tumbled in her gut. Practical. Not feel. How long will it take us? she said loudly as the light changed and the car lurched forward. A half hour only, Mrs. As long as we have no more idiots like this one. The driver flung his hand against the window as though ready to seize the other by the throat. But his eyes sparkled, his glance was lively – he would feast on this for days, his duel with an ignorant man, how he had dealt with him, how he had shown him what was what. While she was forced to sit and be driven through a darkening city as her brother tumbled soundlessly out of the sky, over and over, only the angle of his body changing against the light.

The cab driver in Vancouver was quiet, half asleep in fact, slumped heavily against the door as he drove with two fingers on the wheel. The raw-cheeked toddlers dreamt of rocking horses and milk and biscuits as the empty black streets hissed under the tires. Her seatmate on the plane, a white-haired woman in her fifties, had spoken of the married daughter she was travelling to visit, such a long way, the grandchildren's faces different every time she saw them. The baby's six months old already, I can't wait to see her. Do you have children? The last time I came Craig had just learned to walk up the stairs by himself. There's the oddest smell of oil paint, have you noticed?

Richard, tumbling out of the sky, turned impish, grinning. I'm a portrait painter, she said. I specialize in corpses. She saw herself fanged and clawed, saw the woman's face blink and crumple and look down at her tray. Oh why had she shattered those building blocks and lullabies, let in this icy wind? Richard flew grinning past the window of the plane. She was pleasant, she was harmless, but I snarled, I bit. How many lives will you take with you, Richard? Answer me that. She might have held me like a daughter, stroked my hair, said How awful, is there anything, poor dear. Instead a wave of cold lapped now between her and this stranger whose own children did not dance on rooftops or travel round the country in paint-splashed clothes. The woman did not speak to her again. The cab driver too had lost the power of speech. She travelled in the country of the blind and mute towards Richard, white and silent somewhere in a dark room. Past that building, and that, and that, dim blocks in the rain and dark – had he jumped there, or there? She was too cold ever to be warmed again. In Toronto there were familiar voices, lighted rooms, her desk, plants, the phone ringing. The half-painted ceiling. Richard had crossed the continent in a single leap. She could only fol-low in her blind earthbound fumbling way, a mole nosing up towards light. They were on a bridge now and there were lighted towers ahead. She was suddenly seized like a child with homesickness. She would venture out on a limb of words. Is it far to the hotel? she asked, her voice cracking. *Yes no maybe so* came back like an echo from a childhood game, the skipping rope snapping at her ankles. *Yesnomaybeso. Yes no may –* Richard. No. No. No.

Practical. Not feel. She moved, spoke, smiled, held room keys and luggage, said Yes please and No thank you. Someone else held frozen hands under the hot water tap in her room, splashed her face. In the hallway one of the underwater people went by, whistling. She knocked on Edward's door and in the silence saw the open window, the empty room, the curtains fluttering. Edward, Eddie, she said, possibly out loud; the door opened and Edward stood there, solid and balding in his shirt-sleeves and stocking feet. She held her arms out then, pressed her face into a smell of sweat and laundered cotton and shav-ing lotion. Firm, in command, invigorating, the smell on which empires had been founded, oceans subdued. Which in fact left little time for hand-holding. Martin had smelled like this, and her father, even on his mornings after, standing there swaying slightly before he left for work. She was three years older and two inches taller, but she let Edward take her by her shaking arm and guide her to one of the beds. He placed a glass of something in her hand and she drank. A tiny flame trickled into her stomach and burned there, steadily. Edward smoked, dropping ash on the carpet. A flock of Canada geese flew improbably across the pale gold wallpaper.

I thought you'd stopped, she said.

I did. Three months ago. Started again on the plane.

He must have brought the Scotch for her. He never drank, not even champagne at family birthdays. Like him to remember to put a bottle in his suitcase. At those same celebrations Richard stood on a chair and recited The Cremation of Sam McGee or The Walrus and the Carpenter by heart. Never swayed or slurred his words but held himself a little too upright, walked a little too carefully. Smoked Gitanes or sucked breath mints so you could never be sure.

The first thing I thought when I saw the cop was Mark. Shoplifting candy or something. Edward stubbed out his cigarette.

Was he drunk?

His blood alcohol reading was the equivalent of two beers.

Not that that answers anything.

Then he said Richard and I thought, that bike. That bloody bike.

My hands went numb after you called. They're like ice.

He had an accident last year, did you know? Edward took one of her hands and pressed it against his side, the warmth seeping through like a stain. Didn't tell Mom, of course.

Have you phoned?

No.

Edward the messenger. Hey, ma, your kid's dead. Richard on that Sunday school picnic capering perilously close to the cliff edge above the creek, the school superintendent yelling at him from the firepits. Later at eighteen grinning at her from his hospital bed, three broken ribs and a fractured fibula after he'd rolled their mother's car driving home from a party, four months after their father's death. Still later he'd collided with a logging truck in Oregon, a taxi in Winnipeg. Walked away from everything. We regret to inform you that your son,

Richard Bellamy Logan, was found in the street by a passing –
At least not choked in his own vomit like his father. Or was
that true? No one had actually told her that. Secondhand
deaths, both of them, witnessed by strangers. Not the dignity
of the black-bordered telegram that had come on a bright June
morning to her mother, a bride of a week. We regret to inform
you that Cpl. Robert Edward Bellamy was killed in action in
France on May 3, 1944. There among the lush roses of her parents' garden, the hum and buzz and bird-song of June, standing
weeping beside her new husband for her favourite brother.

What are you going to tell her?

I don't know. Edward took another cigarette from the package beside him on the bed. That he fell, I guess.

You're not telling her the truth?

They haven't found a note.

People don't just fall off buildings.

Then I'll say he was pushed.

Let's wait. Till after.

She'll say we should have phoned.

Ringing in the dark in that small neat apartment, her
mother reaching for her ruffled housecoat, stumbling out into
the hall, her voice sleepy, thick, already anxious. Richie. It's
about Richie, Mom. We're calling to tell you – There's been an
accident. He jumped. No, he fell. I'm afraid so, Mom. The one
who was premature, colicky, allergic, held his breath sometimes till he turned purple, the one who talked late and
crawled early and threw temper tantrums, who sang like an
angel and learned how to play gin rummy at five, also was
found smoking one of Uncle Gordon's cigars around the same
age, who stole a goldfish from Mrs. Adams down the street at
seven and broke windows at twelve and at fourteen discovered
that under its hood a car had a beating heart that could be
taken apart and mended and made to beat again. An accident.
Just stepped off a building.

I'll call, she said.

She'll want to know what the cop said. Edward picked up
the phone and dialled. Again she would have to watch the
slow climb up the stairs, hear the crunch of gravel on the roof,
feel the wind as he spread his arms. The sleeping animal

stirred, kneading its paws in her belly. The twins lay flushed in sleep, the woman on the plane rocked her new grandchild, the teenage girls giggled in their sleeves. Ruthless savages, all of them. Why couldn't it have been a nice death? A death one would be proud to show off to friends. Not for Richard, not even for her mother, but for herself. You didn't tell your colleagues and acquaintances that your father died in a Skid Row rooming house, alone except for a litter of bottles, three days before his fifty-seventh birthday. She could place Richard on a motor-cycle, give it a gentle push, wave just before he turned the corner and vanished from sight.

There's no answer, said Edward.

Maybe she's at the Leuwins' for the weekend.

Guess I'll have to try later.

I'll call a cab, Maureen said.

They held hands like children as they followed the blue-shirted man down the long fluorescent-lit corridor. Are you sure you wouldn't prefer to watch on the colour monitor? he said, opening a door. Moustache, large ears, a fatherly face – did he go home and hug his wife and children to him after his shift? Bruised of course but the face is intact, he said. Maureen wanted to lean forward into the rumpled shirt, against the pocketful of pens over his heart. Empires had been founded, oceans subdued. But this expedition, to touch the cold flesh of a brother, did he know what that was like? She had come because she had missed one opportunity; this was her second chance and she must not fail.

Another door opened. They walked ahead of the man into a white and silent room lined with steel drawers. He ran his finger down a row and pulled one out. Maureen let go of Edward's hand and walked forward. There was the humped nose, her father's chin with its old scar, her mother's dark hair now matted above the high forehead. But also the mouth she shared with him crumpled and twisted, a long blackened welt from temple to jaw, an eyebrow encrusted with blood. The blue eyes shut, unseeing. Poor beautiful bruised fragile bones. They had broken and broken and now they would not mend. She wanted to cradle that bruised head, pick him up and rock him the way she had when he was a baby, singing that rhyme – how did it go? – *All around the mulberry bush, The monkey chased the weasel.* She leaned over him and touched his face, as bloodless and cold as a saint's. If only she could warm him, watch the colour return to the lips and the eyelids flutter.... Richard. Richie. It's me, Maureen. Look, Edward's here too, we've come to take you home. But Edward had taken her arm and was saying something as he pulled her to her feet, the drawer was sliding shut. A key turned in a lock and she stood outside, palms on the glass. How cold and lonely it was in there under the lights! Richie, she said, and felt Edward's arm round her shoulder. There's a coffee shop next door, said the blue-shirted man. If you'll come up to the main desk with me you can sign for the keys. His black heelworn shoes stepped easily and solidly one after the other along the glossy linoleum in front of them as she and Edward walked hand in hand back up the corridor. He chose a good building, the man said as they waited for an elevator. Some of them end up quadriplegics.

There must have been, said Maureen. They sat under a pool of light at a grey Formica counter while a small Chinese woman mopped the floor round their stools.

They haven't found one.

But there must be *something*. Richard wouldn't just –

What do you want, a message on the mirror in lipstick?

Maybe they don't know where to look.

They said they searched the place, Maureen.

Maybe he mailed it.

Oh God, I hope not. Not to Mom.

At least we'd know. We'd know why.

The mop slapped back and forth across the floor, the rain beat gently against the steamy windows. It was clear, wasn't it, stepping off a building? Edward was right – what more did she want? She wanted to go back and scream at that bruised white face until it yielded its secret. Something as concrete and touchable as that mop, the mug of coffee, the clock with its knife and fork hands like the clock in Woolworth's where she and Edward had spent Saturday mornings holding shiny quarters in their fists and twirling round on the stools. Drinking milk shakes and daring each other to run out without paying. Edward telling silly jokes and laughing till he choked to make up for their tiptoeing round that morning past the shut bedroom door, their mother red-eyed and silent. In the evenings, Richard upstairs asleep in his crib, they'd watch their mother pace the kitchen, lifting the curtain every so often to look out. They'd hear the car coming up the street, watch as it turned wide of the driveway and ploughed into the snow-thickened hedge. Then backed up, gears grinding, surged forward and rammed into the hedge again. She hadn't had her driver's licence then but she'd gone outside and backed the car out of the crushed bushes, Edward guiding her from behind, while her father staggered up the path and said Next time tell those bloody kids to clear that bloody driveway before I get home.

We were going to go to Mexico together, said Edward. He said I should do a bike trip before I turned forty.

He must have been joking.

No, he was serious. He'd phoned me twice in the last month to talk about it.

And you were actually considering it?

As a matter of fact I'd said yes. I thought it'd be good to do something together.

You were the one who used to lecture him about the bike.

I thought it was dangerous. Turns out that wasn't the problem, was it?

What else did he talk about? she said.

About this village he wanted to go back to. Crumbling white houses and nets drying on the beach.

I meant besides the trip.

Don't you think I've tried to remember? All the way here on the plane I tried. Sitting in that hotel room. The only thing he talked about was the places we could go. The route we'd take.

He must have said something.

Oh God, Maureen. We're back where we started. Edward ran his finger through the wet circle left by his coffee mug. Placed the mug back in the exact centre of its circle and blew

his nose into a napkin, then bent his head as the sound of mop-
ping stopped for a moment and Maureen laid her cheek against
the smooth curve of his skull.

Two white stone lions with cracked paws lay guarding an
empty fountain at the entrance to the building. The west side,
the detective had said, between 3 and 5 a.m. according to
forensics. The side facing the park, then, now just a dark mass
three hundred yards away beyond the streetlights. If the rain
hadn't washed them away they might still be able to see the
chalk marks. A good building, twenty stories, above average
height for the West End. Maureen did not look up. Edward
tried several keys on the key ring before finding the right one,
Maureen huddled beside him under the overhang out of the
driving rain. She half expected the manager to appear and
demand what they were doing at 4 a.m., but they walked
across the faded red carpet to the elevator in silence.

Were you here, ever? she asked as the floors clicked past on
the illuminated sign.

He hadn't moved in yet when I saw him.

He'd talked in the summer about finding this place. It faced
the ocean, he said, it looked out over the beach and the popcorn stands, the seagulls floated beneath his open window. He
had money in his pocket and a month to lie in the sunshine.
She would have to come visit, he said. But she'd already
planned two weeks in the Laurentians – then had met that
photographer, Polish, she'd thought for a while it might –

The elevator bumped to a stop on the eleventh floor. Thick
carpet muffled their footsteps as they walked down the sleeping hallway. She picked up a newspaper from the mat outside
1142 as Edward unlocked the door. Hadn't removed anything,
the detective had said, so little of value. Had dusted the bathroom mirror and the balcony door for fingerprints, routine pro-
cedure. In her purse she felt for the envelope they'd given her
with his wallet, her father's wedding ring, a sheet of paper
they'd found in his handwriting. Looked like a grocery list.
Did it mean anything to her? No.

A jean jacket hung from a hook inside the door, just above
the bike on its kickstand, a scratched black helmet strapped to

a handlebar. She ran her fingers over the saddle, the smooth metal carapace. Richard didn't trust underground parking lots. In the kitchen several empty mugs cluttered the sink. An opened cereal box stood on the table, a half-eaten bowl of hardened cereal beside it as though he'd been summoned midway through breakfast.

In the living room there was an overstuffed velvet couch, a couple of her mother's appliquéd cushions, a small TV. Books on motorcycle maintenance, back roads of the Pacific Northwest, philosophy. A litter of maps on the coffee table: British Columbia, Alberta, Washington state. She picked one up and saw a faint red pencil line running along the barred black and white secondary roads in a lazy meandering circle. A plan, or was it a trip he'd made already? And a guidebook to Mexico with a photograph stuck between curling pages, Richard and a young woman she didn't recognize, blue sky and a mountain peak in the background.

Nothing out of the ordinary, nothing at all. What had she expected? Edward didn't recognize the young woman either. Yes, there might have been a girl last summer, Richard had mentioned something, Eileen or Ellen. The back of the photograph was blank. You might have paid attention, she said.

What for? In case this happened?

Maybe he told her something.

There was always a girl. It never lasted.

I didn't know about this one.

She studied the photograph again. The woman's blonde hair blew across her face as she squinted into the sun. Richard was tanned, relaxed, smiling, his arm round her shoulder, helmet snug under his armpit. Where were they? Had they been happy? In love? He would stand here forever in the sunlight beside this mountain, relaxed, smiling, on a journey. She tried to decipher the brand name on the helmet before putting the photo in her purse.

She found Edward in the bedroom going through the drawers. I feel funny, doing this, he said. Like a spy. He threw a shirt back on the pile. I don't even know why I'm doing it. The futon on the floor was made up, unslept in. The window overlooked the wet street, parked cars, an identical building across the way, the dark mass of the park in the distance. Even as she heard Edward's voice behind her she felt herself rise and hover several feet above the ground, and then she had slipped through the ceiling and stood looking out over the roof, the streets, the park, towards the mountains outlined by the bleached light of dawn. A breeze lifted the hair from her neck, the air on her cheek was damp. No sound except a bird somewhere, the hushed and sleeping city at her feet. There had been no clatter of metal, cries of bystanders, the distant yowl of an ambulance. Instead a gaze over rooftops, the ocean, stars paling in the light leaking from the horizon. Perhaps an intake of breath. Then air, nothing but air, trusting it as his jacket belled out and he floated there above the earth among the astonished seagulls. She dropped back through the ceiling so quickly she buckled at the knees and staggered into Edward.

Are you all right? You've gone white as a sheet.

She was sick in the toilet while Edward went for a glass of water. She sat on the couch and held the glass tightly, unable to stop shivering. She had stood where he had stood twenty-four hours before, in the dawn light on that rooftop, and had seen only paling stars, a faded moon, the dark shapes of buildings edged in light. This had been her last chance, and she had failed.

It's probably the jet lag, said Edward, and that Scotch. Let me get you some more water.

She looked up at the ceiling again, half expecting a shower of plaster dust. Edward, who believed ceilings were solid, held out the glass. How solid he himself looked standing there, made of dense and reassuring flesh. She wanted to reach out and touch him, she wanted to tell him – what? She was a messenger without a message. Instead she drank the water obediently and watched as Edward folded up the scattered maps and arranged them in a neat pile on the coffee table.

Under a rain-washed sky a bellhop beginning his shift stood yawning by the luggage trolley and a man in a white cap carried crates of milk from a dairy truck to a side entrance. I've got a flight at noon, said Edward. Maybe I can catch a couple hours' sleep.

It's nearly ten in Charlottetown.

I'm too exhausted. I'll call her from home.

She stripped to her underwear and lay between the smooth cold sheets, but the room swam in grey light and floated on a current of voices, car horns, engines. She knocked at Edward's door in her bathrobe. I can't sleep, she said.

You need some rest. Edward turned on the bedside lamp and sat up.

I keep seeing his face.

You have to stop blaming yourself.

I keep thinking that if I knew why, I'd stop seeing him.

There's nothing else we could have done, Maureen.

Nights when they'd lain listening to the shouts downstairs, the crash of something against a wall, she'd tiptoed down the hall to Edward's room. Moving by touch in the darkness, neither of them saying anything, she'd climbed into his bed and they'd lain side by side, a line of warmth between them where their pyjamas met. She climbed into Edward's bed now as he moved to make room for her and they lay together in the semi-dark.

There's this wonderful beach he told me about, said Edward. Goes on for miles. Palm trees and a patio right on the beach where you can drink margaritas out of pineapple shells. They moved closer and lay with their arms round each other, pillowed on sand.

The one with the starfish? she said. He told me about fat purple starfish on a postcard once.

The waves wash them right at your feet. Sometimes the spray splashes you as you sit on the patio.

There they were, her brothers, Edward in his suit and Richard in his leather jacket, sipping their drinks under a sun so bright that when she looked again she couldn't see them. She gazed out at the bright blue ocean and saw two figures swimming through the waves, racing each other to a break-water a hundred yards offshore. She shaded her eyes and saw Richard, she was sure it was him, haul himself dripping from the water and stand glistening in the sunlight. The second figure reached the breakwater, took Richard's extended hand and stood up, still in his suit and miraculously dry. Richard punched him lightly on the shoulder and they both turned to look at something against the horizon. On the patio a waiter cleared away the drinks, and several small children clambered over the bike where it leaned against a palm tree, tracing their initials on dusty metal.

ACKNOWLEDGEMENTS

A BOOK, like condensation, forms in the cold and requires the warm breath of others to help bring it into being. In particular I would like to thank Don Coles; John Metcalf; Carole Glickfeld and the other members of the Touchstone Writers Group; Aron Senkpiel; and my former colleagues and students at Yukon College. A special thank you to Erling Friis-Baastad, for companionship on the journey.

Prof. T.W. Machan of Marquette University kindly provided the Old Norse translation. I owe a particular debt to Urszula Zieliński, who so patiently answered all my questions about Polish names, customs, and history.

I would also like to thank Mary Raines and the Writer-in-Residence Programme of the Libraries and Archives Branch, Department of Education, Government of Yukon, for an enjoyable and productive residency.

For their financial support I would like to thank the Banff Centre for the Arts, the Yukon Advanced Artist Awards (Yukon Lotteries), and The Canada Council.

ABOUT THE AUTHOR

PATRICIA ROBERTSON was born in England, near Manchester, and grew up in Kitimat, B.C. She received her MA in Creative Writing from Boston University in 1983. Her work has appeared in *Quarry*, *Matrix*, *Room of One's Own*, *Canadian Fiction Magazine* and *The Malahat Review* and was singled out by Leon Rooke for inclusion in *The Second Macmillan Anthology*. She has also had a radio play, *Marjorie's War*, produced by CBC's *Morningside*.

She has lived in Madrid, the Canary Islands, London, Vancouver, and the Yukon, where she served as writer-in-residence for the Yukon public library system, taught creative writing at Yukon College in Whitehorse, and co-edited *Writing North: An Anthology of Contemporary Yukon Writers*. She currently lives in Victoria where she is a freelance writer and editor.

Typeset in Trump Mediaeval,
printed and bound by The Porcupine's Quill, Inc.
The stock is acid-free Zephyr Antique Laid.